ROCKET TO A NEW HIGH IN THRILLS AND EXCITEMENT WITH
MIKE MARS—ASTRONAUT

Join Mike Mars—America's newest space-hero—in the first of his adventures on Project Quicksilver.

Mike's life-long dream is to become an astronaut and lead America's race to the stars. But he swiftly finds that secret forces are determined that he never reach his goal. Risking his life at every turn, Mike discovers that his enemy seems to be one of his fellow astronauts!

And don't miss MIKE MARS FLIES THE X-15, also published this month.

D1059873

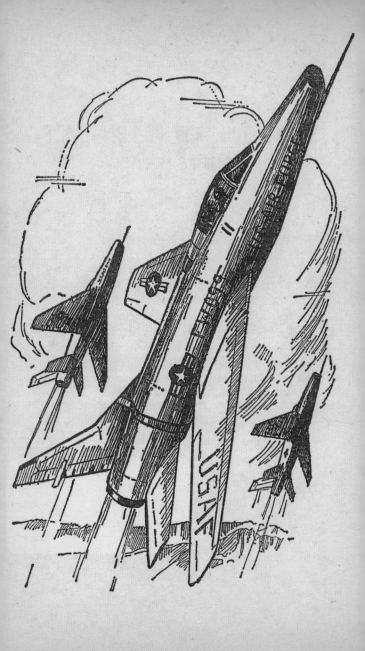

MIKE MARS ASTRONAUT

by DONALD A. WOLLHEIM

Illustrated by Albert Orbaan

PAPERBACK LIBRARY, Inc.
New York

Dedicated to all the brave men of the United States who fought in the air to make this planet fit for the rest of us to live in, and in particular to the memory of my dear friend and kinsman

ALFRED W. ROSS

T/Sgt., U.S.A.A.F.; born 1923, died in combat 1944.

The author wishes to extend his personal gratitude for the valuable assistance rendered him in the course of preparing this book by the United States Air Force and by the National Aeronautics and Space Administration. In particular, thanks are due to Capt. James C. Sparks, Jr., of the USAF New York Information Office, to Capt. Oliver N. Jackson, 14th Fighter Group, to Edward H. Kolcum, Press Information Officer of N.A.S.A., and to the I.S.O. staff of Tyndall Air Force Base, headed by Col. Broun H. Mayall.

CONTENTS

CHAPTER 1

MARS ONE ON THE BEAM

"Mars 1 to Base. Mars 1 to Base. Mission completed. Am returning to field with empty racks, low tanks, high hearts. Do you hear me? Over."

A line of four jet-fighter planes was roaring its way high in the clear cloudless air above the Nevada desert. The speaker, strapped in beneath the clear transparent canopy of his U. S. Air Force F-100, looked for all the world like a man from Mars.

NO STEP — WARNING — NO STEP

"Mars 1 to Base."

His head was covered by a deep-set gleaming white helmet, on the front of which was the white star and blue circle of the service to which he belonged. His eyes were covered by thick goggles; his nose and mouth were concealed from view by the rubbery mask and nozzle of his oxygen supply. For up here, the air was far too thin to permit unprotected breathing.

His hands rested lightly on the controls of his pulsing and powerful little ship. His eyes turned momentarily toward the speed indicator—the fast jet was traveling beyond the speed of sound, past the sound barrier. His spirits were high and soaring even faster than his ship, for this was a big day for Mike Mars and his friends.

"Base to Mars 1. I hear you loud and clear. Come right on in. And no fooling. Do you get me?"

Mike's face broke into a wide smile, invisible beneath the mask, but there. "I get you," he said into his throat microphone, "loud and clear, too. No fooling around . . . but maybe a little extra maneuvers. In line of duty, you might say, eh? Over and out."

The plane roared along, followed in precise wingtip-on-wingtip formation by the three other ships of this team, designated by the name of the red planet. Mars 1, which was the leader, piloted by the speaker mentioned above, suddenly waggled his stubby wings. Mars 2, following right behind, waggled his. Promptly Mars 3 took up the signal and Mars 4, following in the rear, waggled right afterward.

"Mars 2 to Mars 1," came in over Mike's tightly padded earphones within the confinement of his helmet. "Lead on. Wahoo!"

Mike smiled. Scrawled on the brim of his hard white helmet, just beneath the insignia, were four letters, his initials: M.A.R.S. This was his lucky marking, his initials, his nickname, and naturally the code name of his pilot-training team at good old Nellis Air Force Base. He didn't have to look back to know what Mars 2 would look like.

Mars 2, his best friend in the couple of years of hard training they had gone through together to become pilots of jet planes, would look exactly like him in his cockpit. Mars 2 would be in the same kind of bundled-up, padded, and tightly encased flying suit, with the same kind of parachute strapped to his seat. He'd have an oxygen mask, too, and goggled eyes and a white helmet. But a little blue feather would be sticking jauntily out of the side of his helmet, held on by a strip of Scotch tape. That was Johnny Bluehawk's mark.

Now Mike Mars twisted his controls, set his lips in a sharp smile. The trim silvery ship with the bright orange wing tips neatly rolled over, barrel-rolled like a corkscrew angling through the thin air. Right behind him, Johnny Bluehawk rolled over in turn. Then Marty Sherrod, next in line, slid his wings over and turned upside down and back again. Finally, in neat precision, Rod Harger corkscrewed and straightened back.

Then Mike flipped his wings again, and sharply dipped the speedy silver thunderbolt down. Down he plunged, as if about to bury his Super Sabre, like a meteor into the bleak inhospitable landscape of the rolling Nevada wilderness. After him, right on his heels, came Johnny and Marty and Rod, like four mighty roaring hawks plunging on some yet invisible and helpless chicken.

Indeed, had there been anyone below to witness them, he would have been paralyzed by fear. The sudden rushing appearance of the four silvery jets, with their billowing trails of white smoke, and the accompanying roaring thunder of their powerful engines, would have left anyone standing in their path speechless. But nothing lived down there that would be bothered for long.

Out across the vast uninhabited land that made up the training grounds of one of America's largest airfields, Nellis in Nevada, there were no towns, no people to be terrified by the rushing and roaring of the engines, by the terrible crash of the sound barrier being shattered, which happened not once but many times a day over this desolate terrain. A few rattlesnakes, some scurrying lizards seeking cover in clumps of scattered sage, hairy land spiders who could sense the onrushing peril only through the vibrations of the ground—that was the total of the natives of this region.

But the four planes did not crash. One after another they pulled their noses up, swooped close to the ground, and rocketed upwards on clouds of suddenly black smoke. In his cockpit Mike Mars felt the pressure of his rise pushing against him, but he didn't mind. This was a big day for him and the others.

It was the last day of his F-100 training. Tomorrow was graduation day for this class. In a few days more they'd be ready for the next exciting assignment, for more powerful planes, for permanent stations, perhaps on foreign shores or distant bases.

One after another the four reached their original height, leveled off, and headed south. The radio beam came to life in Mike's ear. "Base to Mars 1. Base to Mars 1. Stop horsing around. Come in direct. Now. This is orders. I repeat, Mike, cut it out!"

Mike laughed at the speaker's break in code usage. "I hear you," he said. "This is Mars 1, coming in."

The four shot off in a direct line. In a few minutes the long runways of their home base could be seen laced like tiny webs across the grayish ground of the land far below. Mike waggled his wings, and the four circled around in a long, low spiraling loop, cutting speed and coming closer and closer. Then, with the landing field a mere two or three miles away and looming clear, Mike executed a sideslip, and swung down.

One after another, Johnny, Marty, and Rod peeled off to follow him down.

They came into the landing strip one after another, neat and clean. As each ship rolled down the wide, flat runway, it discharged a small parachute from its rear, which bellowed out immediately and dragged the fast ship back so that at long last each silvery thunderbolt came to a halt at the farthest end of the landing strip. Then, puffing invisible low-powered jets, the four taxied around, rolled rumbling and grumbling back to their proper stations on the main field of the base. Only after they had been jockeyed back into position, guided by the waving hands of their ground crew chiefs, did the jets cut out, cease their angry grumbling at having to come down, and go to rest.

Around each ship the men of the servicing crews raced up. Ladders were set against the cockpits, whose hoods had already been thrust back. Willing hands helped each of the four very young pilots to climb out; and after their reports had been handed in, the four finally made their way to the Base Operations building.

As the four walked across, a man in the light khaki uniform of a ground officer came to meet them. He reached them, a broad smile on his face. "Congratulations, boys," he called as he came close. "I hear tell you all made a perfect score on the targets again."

Mike Mars smiled broadly. His keen gray eyes twinkled merrily. "Yes sir, we sure knocked 'em out." With his helmet off and held loosely in the crook of his arm, his unruly shock of sandy hair gave a specially youthful touch to his walk. The freckles that bridged his nose wrinkled up in his smile, for he knew what was coming.

"But I also hear that you spent some extra gas on your way back, in spite of what the tower said," went on Major Killinger, who was their official instructor and commander. He drew his eyes down in what was meant to be a stern frown. At any other time, this would have caused the four young pilots alarm, but not this afternoon. This was special.

"Sorry, sir," said Mike, adopting the same pseudo-serious tone. "We saw some rattlesnakes that needed shaking up, sir."

14

The major broke into a chuckle, slapped the now laughing youth on the back. "This time we'll overlook it, eh? Get out of those togs, get something to refresh yourself, and when you have time, look in on my office. There may be something of interest there."

He turned and went off, while the four went on to the main operations building, checked in their flying equipment, and retired to the little canteen room.

Mike drew himself a glass of milk and a doughnut and carried it over to the table where the other three had located. Johnny Bluehawk was sipping a bottle of pop, his deep black eyes staring thoughtfully at Mike as he walked over. Johnny was a striking figure of a young fellow. His hair was close cropped and jet black. His skin was an unusual ruddy tan; his nose was sharp and slightly curved. He was an Indian, a Cheyenne from Montana, and Mike was proud to call him his best friend. In a way the two complemented each other— Johnny serious and taut as a bowstring, Mike loose and laughing and quick as an arrow.

Rod Harger set down a cup of coffee and reached for a cigarette. His pale blue eyes looked up as Mike sat down. "What do you suppose the major's got for us?" he asked. His voice was low and cool, and his round pale face reflected no anxiety, though he apparently felt it.

"What's the difference?" said the fourth of their party, Marty Sherrod. "Probably a citation for having completed the F-100 training course. I think I'll go and see, anyway." Marty, a tall, lanky young man, got up and sauntered out.

Mike gulped his milk. "It seems like yesterday," he said slowly, "that we first got here. Yet now we've passed this step of our training. Feels real good; deep down real good."

Harger and Bluehawk nodded, and the Cheyenne added, "First, the T-33's, then the T-37's, and then our lieutenant's bars. Now that the supersonic jets are mastered, I guess we're ready for the Starfighters and the Delta-wings, and someday the real rocket jobs."

Mike finished his milk, sat back. "I can't wait. I can see them now," he said. "The big sleek F-104's, just waiting for us to get in and ride them. But it's the rocket jobs I'm really hoping for." He leaned forward, his eyes creased in earnest eagerness. "You know, each step, each bit of training is another step up the ladder. Someday we're going right on up, out of the atmosphere, into space, right up there to the moon

15

and the planets and the stars. It'll be somebody like us that'll do it. Some fellow maybe our own age."

Rod Harger smiled a tight private smile and nodded ever so slightly. Johnny Bluehawk just shrugged.

Johnny Bluehawk   *Rod Harger*

Marty Sherrod was back, dashing into the canteen as if he'd run all the way from the major's office. He caught his breath and started talking even as he plunked himself down into his seat. "You know what! They're looking for astronauts! They're setting up a space-flight training program—and we can all register for it. Right now! It's posted on the wall in the major's office—and most of the gang is right there now filling out the forms!"

Mike Mars

"Wow!" shouted Mike, jumping up. "Let's go! That's it!
Come on, fellows, next stop the moon!"

And the four dashed out.

CHAPTER 2

VOLUNTEERS FOR SPACE

THERE was already a large group of fellows gathered around the bulletin board outside the major's office. As Mike Mars and his teammates entered, the place was buzzing with excited comments, discussion, even arguments, as their classmates thrashed out the merits and demerits of the news. Mike pushed his way through the crowd and, with Johnny and Rod at his heels, managed to get close enough to read the sheet of paper posted there.

"Space Task Group," read Johnny over his shoulder. "What's that?"

"It's part of the National Aeronautics and Space Administration. See up in the corner of the letterhead. That's the special board the government set up to organize and direct our American program for conquering space," Mike explained, and read on.

As his eyes went over the several short paragraphs, he couldn't help but exclaiming, "Gee, they are looking for volunteers to go into outer space. They want members of this class, and others who are just getting their final training."

Rod, looking at the paper over Mike's other shoulder, had a strange look on his face, a thin-lipped stare of concentration. He offered no comment, but read to himself. Mike and Johnny, on the other hand, were gasping out to each other the possibilities—just as most of the young pilots were doing.

"It warns that the training will be hard and that the ones finally selected to be astronauts must be dead serious, must be ready to risk their lives, and must not expect a lot of personal glory," Mike commented. "That makes sense. There's been a lot of glamour attached to space flight, but we know already from just our own training as pilots that it really means concentration and steady nerves."

"I wonder why they want young fellows like us, never assigned to regular Air Force work," said Johnny. "You'd think that really experienced test pilots might work out better."

"Oh," said Mike, "maybe they figure that youth counts and maybe they don't want us to have any preconceived notions."

Rod Harger followed the two away from the board to a corner of the crowded hallway. "I heard that they have a project already going with experienced test pilots. This must be a new development, sort of checking on the other."

Mike nodded. "That's possible. Well, it's our good luck."

Marty Sherrod made his way over to them. "Going to apply for it? The major has the applications ready. All we got to do is fill them out."

"You bet," said Mike, his eyes agleam. "Wild horses couldn't keep me back."

"Me, too," said Johnny and Marty almost in the same breath. As for Rod, he simply started off for the major's office without a word.

As the four crowded in, they found a dozen or so before them. At his desk Major Killinger was handing out a questionnaire to each pilot that came up to him. The four got theirs, made their way out of the little office, and found a table in a nearby room that nobody was using. Draping themselves over it, they applied themselves to filling out the forms.

It began by announcing the formation of a new group to be called Project Quicksilver. The purpose of this project was to select and train seven young men for work in outer space. They were to be trained in space techniques, rocket pilotry, survival in outer space, and finally the manning of vehicles designed to operate in interplanetary space.

This project was restricted to qualified pilots of the Air Force, the Navy, and the Marines, who had mastered the controls of supersonic jet planes but had not yet received permanent assignments to regular service posts. They had to be unmarried and have an excellent record.

The questions were relatively simple and standard. They merely called for the name and personal data of the applicant —his birth, home, education, and training to date. There was a large space to be filled in by the base commander with his opinions as to the qualifications of the applicant.

The four filled in their forms carefully. Mike found his heart beating excitedly as he did so. For all his young life he had dreamed of space flight, and now at last it looked as if the opportunity had come. This was an important event in his life, maybe the most important since the day he'd signed up in the Air Force.

Johnny Bluehawk's thoughts were clear and sober. He knew what Mike's ambition was and he went along with it. He was himself a member of the original Americans, the Indians, and he never allowed himself to forget his deep obligations to his people. For him, there could be no question as to whether he should try out for this. If an Indian, a "redskin," could be among the pioneers of space exploration, it might do a good deal to assist his people to regain the dignity they had lost in the loss of their ancestral lands.

Marty Sherrod was also excited, much as Mike was, but to him this was a big adventure. It sounded like a terrific thing, a chance to visit the moon and Mars and the other exciting planets. He'd do his best to win that ticket.

What Rod Harger was thinking was never stated to his teammates, but he filled out his application with grim attention. In the back of his mind he saw the power and the glory that would attend the first man to reach the moon. He saw the world full of admiration for a stocky, pale-eyed, pale-haired hero named Rodney Harger, Jr. In the back of that mental image his mind always saw the shadowy figure of another man, an older, gray-haired version, also coldly pale—Rodney S. Harger, Sr.—who had stood behind his son all the way and had pointed to glory.

When the forms had been completed, the four made their way back. As Mike went to the major's desk and handed his form in, the major smiled at him. A pile of similar applications were already on his desk. "I'm glad to see you trying out for this, Mike," he said. "With your record here, you ought to be a cinch."

Mike smiled shyly. He was always embarrassed at this sort of thing. He tried his best as a matter of principle. He was always surprised when somehow his best turned out to be all too often the very best. Long ago, when he was a little kid, his father had told him, "If you're going to do a thing, do it right or don't do it at all. And if you do it right, you'll never have anything to worry about."

Throughout his life Mike had always stuck to this principle, and it had proved to be good advice. Doing things right was his whole secret—it was strange how many people, with the best of intentions, didn't quite follow through all the way on anything.

"I hope so, major," Mike said. "This could be just the thing I'm looking for."

Major Killinger nodded. "These applications will go out today. We expect to have notification of those accepted in four days."

Rod pushed past Mike and handed his application in, closely followed by the other two.

At Nellis Air Force Base they had just completed the thirty-day course in the flying of the fast Super Sabre F-100's, the first of the supersonic jets. They had all been graduated as cadets only the month before, receiving their wings and their commissions. Nellis was a stopgap, a necessary postgraduate course.

From there each new pilot would be assigned to a permanent base in one of the many Air Force posts around the United States or wherever else the necessities of defense had placed our fliers, such as the famed Thule base in northern Greenland, the hot sands of the Libyan desert, the valleys of Old Spain, amid the ancient cities of West Germany, the hamlets and vales of Merry England, the bleak areas of Iceland, and the exotic isles of the far Pacific.

The next morning the exitement of the space flight project was temporarily set aside for the excitement of the special graduation ceremony. There was a dress parade behind the base band, which was made up of the regular enlisted airmen whose station was at Nellis. The new class of pilots, now graduates of the short, intense course, stood at attention while the colonel made a brief speech.

They were reminded again of the tradition of the United States Air Force and of the two years of training they had already undergone before receiving their wings. They were reminded of what they had all come to know firsthand during the hectic past few weeks—that Nellis was one of the toughest courses in air combat training in the corps, that on this day of graduation they had proved themselves first-class jet-fighter pilots. "Now," the colonel went on, "you will await your next assignment, the call that will put to practical use in the defense of our nation all that has gone before. I wish you all God-speed."

The brief ceremony over, the men found themselves with several days of ease. Many of the fellows went into town to Las Vegas and had themselves a good time. But Mike found himself too restless for that. In his mind, over and over again, he thought of the meaning of Project Quicksilver. The Space Age was dawning and he could be a part of it. He realized how deeply he wanted this.

He spent the next days reading and rereading all he could on the subject. He and Johnny took long walks, talking about the possibilities of the thing.

"With the earth satellites and the rocket missiles, Atlas and all that, the day of real manned space flight is very close," Mike said on one of their walks. "It's going to be one of us that

They were first-class jet pilots.

does it. The fellows who are still in school now, the boys of ten, eleven, twelve, and on, some of them will be the men who man the future spaceships. There's a whole new frontier to open up, and it's opening up now. We're pretty lucky to be on hand."

Johnny nodded. "Yes, that's so. The world is going to be a lot different in the next twenty or thirty years. It's a very sobering thought to think that we might have the chance of being among those who make it so. It's sort of deep, like thinking of God or being in church. It makes you feel small and humble to be waiting at the door of infinite space."

"That's how I've always felt, deep down," Mike said. "This is a bigger thing than anybody's personal ambitions."

It was three mornings later when Rod Harger, who had gotten up, washed, and dressed earlier than the others, came back from a prebreakfast visit to the major's office. He banged on the doors of all the fellows on his floor of the officers' quarters. "I've got the orders from the Space Task Force," he called out. "You fellows for Project Quicksilver come and get them!"

In a moment the hall was filled with clamoring pilots. Harger had a batch of envelopes in his hand; he read out the name on each, handing them out. There was an envelope for Johnny and one for Marty Sherrod; one obviously addressed to himself was sticking out of his blouse pocket. Mike Mars waited for his, but the little pile of envelopes diminished and was gone. His name had not been called. He looked startled.

Going up to Rod, he asked, "Anything for me?" Rod looked back at him. "Sorry, Mike, I didn't see any with your name on it. Guess it may be coming later."

Mike swallowed his confusion and disappointment, went over to Johnny and read the orders that were contained in Johnny's envelope. It was a short simple directive.

Addressed to John Bluehawk, it said, "Your application for Project Quicksilver has been accepted. You are to report promptly at 10 A.M. to the School of Aviation Medicine, Randolph A.F.B., San Antonio, Texas." The reporting date was three days away. A final note added, "Failure to report on time will be counted against your examination record and may disqualify you."

Mike drifted about, asking the others. Four of the applicants had been politely turned down. The others, eight in all, had been accepted, Rod and Marty among them.

But there had been no reply at all for Mike Mars. Did this mean he had been rejected?

CHAPTER 3

PLEDGE TO THE RED PLANET

MIKE quickly finished dressing, washed, and left for Major Killinger's office without waiting for breakfast. The major wasn't in, but his assistant said he was at the mess hall, so Mike went down there. The major, who like so many Air Force men was not at all a stern old-timer, was eating at a table by himself.

When he saw Mike anxiously striding in, the major waved to him and asked him to join him for breakfast. After Mike had ordered, he turned to meet his instructor's shrewd eyes. "I guess I was turned down by the Project Quicksilver committee," Mike said, trying not to show his disappointment.

But it must have showed anyway, for it had been a stunning surprise to find himself left out. The major frowned. "You didn't receive your orders this morning, like the others?"

Mike shook his head. "Nothing. No answer. I assume that means a rejection."

The major shook his head. "Doesn't absolutely. Maybe the orders were delayed for you. Maybe you'll hear later in the day. Sometimes things can get a little mixed up. You *ought* to have been included. Your record was excellent and I gave you a big boost in my report."

Mike smiled a little bit. "I appreciate that. Maybe they thought I was too good for a dangerous project like space-rocket riding. Maybe they want to keep me on jet fighting."

The major thoughtfully shoveled a forkful of eggs into his mouth and Mike followed suit. Then, after swallowing, he said, "That's always possible, but I still think you should get a positive response." He went on eating in silence for a while, then looked up again, and obviously tried to change the subject.

"How did you ever get so tied up with the name Mike Mars?"

Mike finished his eggs, sat back in his chair, and began to sip his milk. "I guess I've always been called that," he began.

He thought back on it. "I think when I first started going to school—well, maybe after I'd learned to read anyway, I started to put my initials on my schoolbooks and my lunchbox and

24

The red planet

stuff. You know, comes out to be M.A.R.S. So that reads Mars and that's what the other kids started to call me.

"I sort of kept on doing it ever since, that's all, I guess," he finished, a little shyly.

But he thought to himself that that wasn't really the whole story. He'd done it deliberately, he realized, since he was about twelve years old.

Mars had at first been a planet to him that was sometimes featured in comic-magazine stories or in science fiction tales. It sounded like fun to have a nickname and since his initials spelled that, it was nice to be called Mike Mars. Better than Shorty or Lefty or Stinky or something like that.

So he had stuck his initials on everything he owned, and had been doing that since he was maybe eight or nine. He'd written it in his school notebooks and on the side of his baseball bat. He'd inked it on his football helmet and on his sweatshirt; he'd chalked it on sidewalks when the other kids were fooling around the same way. Once he'd carved it on the face of his desk—and had been kept after class when the teacher found out.

But then sometime in his twelfth year he had really become interested in astronomy. He'd taken out all the books that had anything to do with astronomy that were available in the local library in the small Midwestern city he lived in. While he didn't understand much of the mathematics that many of these books had to deal with, he was fascinated by the descriptions of the other planets of our solar system. He read about mysterious Venus, the Evening Star that is the closest major planet to our own Earth, and wondered what really was hidden underneath its cloudy blanket.

He read about little Mercury, whirling around so close to the sun, baked and boiling on one side and eternally frozen on the other. He read about mighty Jupiter with its great gaseous belts and its enigmatic Red Spot, and about spooky Saturn with its strange rings. He read about the Moon, and stared long and fixedly at photographs of its great craters and vast empty sea bottoms, its rugged mountains, and its many mysteries right under the nose of humanity.

Most of all he was gripped by the planet Mars—the red planet that was the next world out from Earth in the sun's family of worlds. He read how some astronomers, like Lowell and Pickering, had been convinced that Mars had canals that must have been built by intelligent beings, and how other astronomers, equally capable, had denied that it had any such things at all. He read all the disputes as to whether the thin spidery lines sometimes seen on Mars were real or imaginary. He read about Mars' vast areas of ruddy desert, its curious regions of changing blue-green that might possibly be patches of vegetation, and its white polar caps, which some said were ice and others claimed were frozen atmosphere.

He couldn't get Mars out of his head. For weeks after his discovery of the astronomy books, he sat in class and dreamed of Mars and flying there. He wanted to set foot on that world and see for himself. He wanted so hard to *know*, just to *know*. Here was a terrific mystery that somehow had to be solved.

So one evening, when he was washing to go to bed, he looked

out the open window and he saw the tiny unblinking pinkish star just visible in the dark night sky. As he looked at it, he felt a sudden feeling of determination, of elation.

He looked at himself in the mirror and he saw that there was a wild light in his eyes that reflected the sudden excitement in his being. He looked back at the red planet, and as its faint distant rays caught his eyes, he said aloud to himself, "I'm going to set foot on you someday. I swear right here and now that I am going to reach Mars before I die. I swear that I am going to do all in my power to cross space and see for myself all that you have to offer. I swear it, *I swear it,* now and forever."

He kept his eyes fixed on the red planet, but the distant gleam never flickered, never answered. When he looked away, he knew he had made a life resolution he would never depart from.

He never had.

From that moment on, his life had been decided. He thought out what he should do to accomplish his desire. He arrived finally at several conclusions.

The first was that he must always keep himself in good physical shape. No man could hope to cross space who was handicapped by a body that had been allowed to get soft by laziness or overindulgence, or had been poisoned by heavy smoking or drinking.

The second was that he must always be proficient in his studies. No man could hope to cross space who was stupid or uninformed or unable to learn new things fast and correctly. He must master his arithmetic and his science studies, for they were the tools that would help him reach his goal.

The third was that he must always keep faith. He must never doubt his future, never give up, never allow defeat or failure to cause him to turn away, but always try again. He must never believe that he couldn't get to Mars.

The fourth was to determine exactly what profession would be the one to lead him to the path of space-flying. This inevitably led him to the career of pilot and the Air Force. Unquestionably space-flying was a logical development of air-flying, and unquestionably the United States Air Force was the pioneer in the mastery of ever greater and faster planes and ever greater heights.

So he steered his course to the Air Force. He built model airplanes and in high school he even flew in a glider that the science class had constructed. He joined the R.O.T.C. and the Air Reserve branch. Then he went to college for two years, after

He had made a life resolution.

which he applied for admission to the Air Force as an officer candidate and trainee pilot.

He had been accepted and then had spent two exciting years being trained in the essentials of aviation, in navigation and engineering, and in the theory of flight. Finally, he had flown— first in propeller-driven planes, then in the famous trainer jets, the T-33 and the T-37.

Through all this he had never forgotten his objective. He had not allowed himself to forget. The initials M.A.R.S., inscribed on everything permissible, were always there, and from the very first his fellow cadets and most of his instructors as well had called him Mike Mars.

When he'd finally received his commission and had been sent to Nellis to master the first of the Air Force's "Century" series of jet fighters, he had at last been able to put his familiar letters on his helmet, on his plane.

From first to last, Michael Alfred Robert Samson had held to his oath of that night when he was twelve. He had kept himself in top shape, he had driven himself to master everything

The symbol for Mars

set before him, he had refused to allow himself ever to believe that he could fail.

But now as he sat in the mess hall, it looked as if he had come suddenly upon a blank wall.

He turned to the major again, his thoughts snapped back to the present. "Do you think an inquiry would help?" he asked.

The major shook his head. "I can put an inquiry through, but you wouldn't get an answer before it would be too late. I understand the fellows called have only three days to get there. I'd guess the Space Task Group doesn't have any time to waste. You know we're in a race with the Russians to conquer space, and it looks like the other side is ahead for the time being. We're going to have to move fast to catch up."

Mike nodded. "Oh, I've no doubt we'll catch up . . . and beat them, too. But, gee, I sure would like to be in there in the race on our side."

Major Killinger shrugged. "Remember, these are only the first. There'll be others, and maybe your turn will come in a couple more years."

They got up and left, the major going to his desk, Mike walking back to the quarters. He found the other fellows, those who had been accepted, busily packing. He wandered into Johnny Bluehawk's room, where his Indian friend was stowing away the last of his clothes.

Johnny paused a moment, noting the obvious disappointment that still showed in Mike's eyes. He went over. "Gosh, Mike, I don't understand it at all. If anybody were accepted, it should have been you. When I get to Randolph, I'm going to ask about your application. Maybe I can talk them into looking it over again."

Mike smiled wanly. "Thanks, but I guess they must have their reasons. By that time I'll have probably gotten my orders for assignment elsewhere. But . . . you go ahead and don't think about me. You go on and become an astronaut. I'll be proud just to have known you."

There were a lot of farewells for Mike, because he was the kind of fellow you liked; even when he topped you in some study or drill, it seemed to be so natural that you didn't resent it at all. All but one man, that is. Rod Harger did not bother to say good-by.

And as Mike walked along to the field where the bus would pick up his ex-comrades to take them to the city and their various methods of travel, he overheard Harger comment to someone else, "I'm not surprised that Samson didn't get called. I never thought he was so hot, myself. In fact, he always gave me a swift pain in the neck. Mars, huh!"

Mike stood and watched the bus pull away, and he thought about that remark. He scratched his head. Could his faith, so firm these many years, in his date with the red planet just have been self-delusion?

CHAPTER 4

FASTER THAN SOUND

THE next two days were very uncomfortable ones for Mike. There were still many fellows of his particular training group hanging around, but they were merely awaiting their regular assignment orders. Mike realized that his own orders would be among them, but he could not feel any enthusiasm speculating about where he would be sent. The others would sit around jawing about their interest in seeing Europe or their hopes to be trained for the new and faster F-102's and F-104's that were replacing the Super Sabres all through the regular Air Force.

Mike found no pleasure in such talk—all he could think of was that first step up the ladder of space and how he would miss it. He could have gone into town with the other pilots, enjoyed himself as they did, since there were no regular missions or assignments at Nellis for any of them, but he could not find the heart for it. He was hoping every hour that he would hear from the Space Task Group and get his chance.

But there was no word. Major Killinger was very considerate of him, offered him several opportunities to take a plane up and just enjoy the experience of tearing through the high air, free as a bird, but Mike didn't feel up to it. He tried reading, did some studying on his aeronautics, wrote a couple of long letters to his parents and to some of his old home-town friends, and waited.

The night before the day Johnny and the others were to report, he got a phone call from San Antonio. He ran to the phone when he was paged. It was Johnny Bluehawk.

"Hi, Mike, any news? We going to see you tomorrow?" Johnny's voice tried to sound cheerful.

Mike grinned forcedly, kept his voice light. "Not a word, Johnny. I guess I'm to come along later. Probably they're saving me for the big jump to the stars a hundred years from now."

Johnny grunted. "I can guess how you feel. As for us, well, you know, we're all sort of excited. We checked in here this morning and we're putting up at the Visiting Officers' Quarters. Weather's hot—Texas you know—but we're getting set. At

31

ten tomorrow we go to bat, and well, who knows? If you get assigned near here, come down and look us up if we're still around."

"Sure will, Johnny," Mike said, now feeling sadder than he had before, though he tried not to let his voice give him away. "I haven't had any travel orders yet, but I may be able to route my trip through San Antone long enough to say hello again—if you aren't already on the way to the moon by then."

"Not a chance, really," said his Indian friend. "It looks as if we're going to be in for some tough physical shakedowns."

After a few more light comments, the call ended. Mike drifted back to his quarters, still feeling the confusion that had come over him at realizing how he had been so strangely left out, without a yes or no.

He went to bed early that night, and probably because of that woke up earlier than usual. He heard the bugle sound in the enlisted men's barracks and the sound, usually far enough away not to disturb him, brought him awake with a strange feeling of urgency.

He sat up in bed, suddenly wide awake. There was something he had to do that morning! He shook his head to clear it, sat back. Yes, it was the feeling that this was the day that Project Quicksilver officially started. He started to get back in bed but realized that he was too upset and wide awake to get any more shut-eye. He arose, dressed, went down to the latrine, and washed.

On his way back he passed the doors that had housed his teammates up to a couple of days ago. He opened the door of the room that had been Johnny Bluehawk's, looked in. It was barren of personal belongings, and the bed was neatly made, awaiting the next man assigned here. There was no memory of his Cheyenne flying friend left.

He opened the door next to it, where Rod Harger had been, looked in. He had rarely been in that room when Rod had been there, for there had never been any great chumminess between them. He recalled Rod's rather unkind remark the day he left.

The room seemed as bare as Johnny's and Mike was about to close the door again when his eye caught a spot of white barely visible in the darkness underneath the dresser. Sloppy clean-up, he thought, and because of his rigid training as a cadet, he entered the room to fish out the offending scrap of paper and deposit it in the wastebasket.

He bent down, picked up the scrap of white. It was an envelope. He was about to toss it away when he caught the name typed on the front: *Lt. M. A. R. Samson.* He stopped stock-still, staring. He turned the envelope over; it was open at the back.

Hastily, with quickly beating heart, he opened the envelope and extracted the folded single sheet of paper within it. He knew at a glance what it would say, and it did: "Your application . . . accepted . . . report . . . promptly at 10 A.M. . . . Randolph A.F.B., San Antonio . . . Failure to report on time . . . may disqualify . . ."

This was his order. How had it gotten here? He remembered that it had been Harger who had brought the orders back from headquarters that day. Had Mike's merely been dropped by accident . . . or was there something more sinister behind the disappearance of this one envelope beneath the bureau here?

Mike glanced at his watch. It was about five minutes after six. He turned, ran back to his room, finished dressing in an-

This was his order!

other minute, and dashed out. He ran down the path to the quarters occupied by the higher officers, found Major Killinger's chambers, and banged on the major's door. In a few moments the major himself stuck his head out, unshaven, just awakened.

Mike excused his haste and when the major, still in pajamas, let him in, Mike showed his his orders and explained where he'd found them. The major was astounded. Then Mike unfolded his plan, pointing to his watch, explaining.

The major drew down his brows in thought, nodded. "There's two hours difference between here and Randolph, you know," he finally remarked. "Ten o'clock there is Central Standard Time. We're on Pacific Standard here. It'd be our eight o'clock that this project starts."

Mike nodded. "Yes, I know that, but . . ." and he insisted. Suddenly the major jumped to a phone. "Blast it, boy, I agree with you. You deserve the chance, and I'm going to bat for you all the way. You go on down to the field as fast as you can get into your flying outfit. I'm calling the colonel right now. I'll be down as soon as I clear it."

As Mike dashed out of the room, he could hear the major's voice raised, excitedly talking to the commanding colonel.

He caught a car going down to the hangars, and reached Base Operations in quick time. Hurrying down to his locker, he hastily climbed into his flying outfit, including G-suit, boots, lined gloves, and parachute and, grabbing his helmet and oxygen mask, he clomped back out to the field.

There were several planes lined on the ramp, for like all bases they were ready at all times. As he went out to the line, the major, still unshaven and wearing coveralls hastily pulled on over his pajamas, came tearing up in a service jeep. As he saw Mike he stood up and waved.

"It's O.K., Mike. The colonel was as mad as the devil when he heard about it. He says go ahead and give her the gun and he'll back you up all the way. And . . . say . . . isn't that the plane you used yourself out there?"

Mike half ran, as best he could in the encumbering high-altitude outfit, toward the sharp-nosed, stubby-winged silver bullet over which the olive-colored coveralls of the ground crew were crawling, putting the ship into commission.

He reached it as fast as the major did. The ground crew men looked at him, and raised a cheer. They had serviced Mike during his training and they all liked him. "The ship's about ready

34

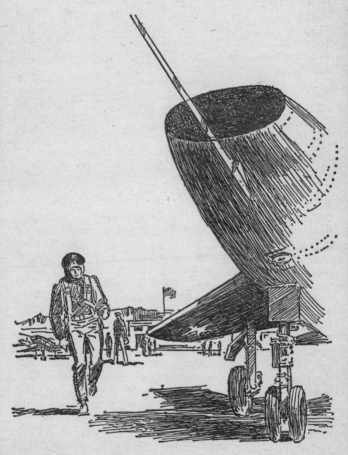

Mike ran toward the silver bullet.

to go, all fueled, sir," said their chief. "Shall we begin the checkout, sir?"

The major looked at his watch. "Half past six," he said. "It's against regulations, but you'd better skip the checking if you want to have a chance."

Mike gritted his teeth. Checking out was all too often a matter of life and death, but he trusted this crew and he knew the ship. "Let's go," he said and climbed the little ladder and let himself down into the narrow confining space of the cockpit.

The canopy came down over him, shut tight. The ground men took the ladder and raced away. Mike turned on the ignition.

The jets caught, the ship trembled to the first surge of power. He glanced over the control dials hastily: all seemed in order, the powerful jet fighter fully fueled.

His radio came to life. "Mars 1 to tower. Ready for take-off."

The tower control responded instantly. "Tower to Mars 1. Cleared for take-off. Take Runway 3."

The jet rolled down the field to the end of the runway, its engine throbbing powerfully. At the end of the runway, Mike glanced once more at the clock on his dial, gritted his teeth, and called out to the tower that he was taking off. "Give her the gun, Mars 1," sang the tower.

The F-100 Super Sabre rolled down the runway, gathering speed steadily. As Mike watched his dials and power, a strange coolness came over him—that same great reserve he knew he could always count on in emergencies. As he reached the right speed, he shoved in his afterburner.

There was a terrific surge of power as the extra blaster on the jet cut in. Mike surged back in his seat and headed the ship upwards. It climbed almost vertically into the air under the terrific stress of its burning exhaust. Up and up Mike went, leveling off finally and heading out across the vast desert expanse of Nevada in a southeasterly direction.

Faster and faster he drove the ship, and he watched its little Mach meter steadily climb towards the strategic moment when the ship would burst the sound barrier.

He glanced down for an instant just before it did and ascertained that there was no town or settlement in sight. He pushed the ship on and the meter registered Mach 1, the speed of sound. Below him the desert must have rocked with the ear-shattering boom of the sonic blast, but there would be no one to hear it.

Now he drove the ship on, faster and faster. He knew it had

36

its limits, but this time he had to find them and hold to them. The cockpit was strangely silent as the speed left his own sound behind, never to catch up. The vibration of the ship was slowly increasing, and Mike knew this was what he had to watch out for. As fine as the F-100 was, it was not able to go too much beyond the speed he had already attained.

Seated in the controls he saw the speed indicator reach 750 miles per hour. He held it there, sped on.

Roaring across the sky, a tiny dot too high up to be seen from below except by the most keen-eyed, he crossed Nevada, bulleted across the Painted Desert, passed the Continental Divide, blazed over the empty stretches reserved for the atomic experimenters of Los Alamos and the rocket men of Holloman, and raced on straight as a bullet through cloudless blue skies towards San Antonio, a thousand miles from Las Vegas.

It was twenty past seven when he crossed into Texan air and picked up the beam. It was a quarter to eight when he got his landing instructions from Randolph Base. It was ten of eight when he came down at a dangerously high speed to race along the runway, depending on his drag parachute to keep his trim plane from overshooting the mark. Even as his wheels raced over the ground, a little red light on his dashboard reminded him that his tanks were completely empty at last.

A little yellow jeep paced his ship to a stop and as he climbed out, at five minutes to eight, the driver raced right up to him and waved a hand to jump in. They were ready and waiting. He leaped into the little car, not waiting to remove his helmet. He knew that the colonel had indeed "gone to bat" for him. His arrival had been expected.

At precisely eight o'clock by Mike's watch, which still ran on Pacific Standard Time, but ten o'clock by the dial of the clock in the lobby of the School of Aviation Medicine, he walked into a small classroom, still wearing his bulky G-suit, still carrying his white helmet with its scrawled letters M.A.R.S. under his arm.

There were about twenty-five young men in the room waiting nervously in their seats. As one they all looked at Mike, and most of them were amazed. But several of them jumped up and yelled. Mike waved as he saw the astonishment on Johnny's coppery face and the equal gapes of amazement on those of his other friends.

As he took a seat, he did not fail to note the look of blank thunderstruck astonishment that distinguished the features of Rod Harger.

CHAPTER 5

PROJECT QUICKSILVER

SILENCE fell over the room as a rather distinguished-looking gray-haired man in civilian clothes came in, accompanied by another man in the uniform of an Air Force colonel. The two mounted the platform at the front of the room. The colonel went up to the speaker's rostrum, waited until he had everyone's attention. His glance swept the room, sizing up the men there. His eyes stopped at Mike, stared at him a long time.

Mike was still in his flying outfit and was already aware of rapidly growing discomfort from this tight, padded, pressurized suit. The colonel's narrow, weathered eyes rested on him; then a slight smile broke over his features.

"I guess we'll have to hold up starting our session here for five minutes while the young man who apparently just flew in from Mars, judging by his outfit and his helmet, can excuse himself long enough to get out of it." He nodded leave to Mike, as the other fellows stared again at him and a wave of titters went over the room.

Mike hastily stood up, grinning broadly, and slipped out the door. Once outside, he hastily unsnapped his suit, climbed awkwardly out of it. He caught the arm of a passing airman, and asked him to check the outfit at the main gate. Then he returned to the room where everyone was waiting and slipped into his seat.

The colonel rapped on the stand again. He became abruptly serious. "Let me start by introducing myself. I'm Colonel Drummond, Otis M. Drummond, and I will be in charge of you during the entire process of selection. This gentleman with me is Dr. Hugo Holderlin, who will be responsible for the first series of examinations you will receive here at this institution. Dr. Holderlin, of whom you may have heard, was one of the founders of the science of aviation medicine and is a director of this school. But before I turn you over to him, I am going to brief you on Project Quicksilver."

He paused, looked around. The room was silent. He nodded to himself, as if satisfied with what he saw, then, clearing his throat, began.

"We all know that mankind stands at the threshold of a new frontier. That is, the frontier of outer space. We have carried aviation right up to the limits of the atmosphere; we are engaged in perfecting the techniques which will carry us beyond.

"I do not have to remind you of the swift advance of rocketry in the past dozen years. You have all grown up with it, and none of you have been unmoved by it. I am sure that since your boyhood days you have followed the news of each new step upwards toward the stars. With the final achievement in the last couple of years of the first actual space vehicles, the Sputniks, our own Explorer satellites and Vanguards, we have at last begun to control the techniques which will eventually allow the exploration and conquest of other worlds.

"Already men are talking of such things as permanent space platforms for the study of our Earth, for the study of the universe, for the transmission of messages and television over a world-wide system, and also for the establishment of new bases for the defense and protection of our freedoms. I can tell you that there are men already at work in this country, in various plants and testing grounds, who are actively designing these platforms, who are working out the details of these manned and robot satellites, of these essential footholds in outer space.

"But each step man takes must be learned. A child does not bounce out of his cradle to run at full speed at once. First he crawls, then he toddles, and only after long and painful effort he masters the art of walking. So it must be with our conquest of space.

"First we have learned how to make the tools that will take us up there. Then we have had to study the problems involved in keeping a man alive in conditions for which nature never designed him. All of you have won your wings as pilots for the Air Force or the Navy. You therefore already know much that has been necessary to make it possible to fly in planes that must surpass the speed of sound. You have learned firsthand something of the dangers of the upper atmosphere, of rapid turns, of the rise and fall of pressure.

"Your knowledge will stand you in good stead, but you will learn more, much more, before your training is over. Because the conditions facing us in outer space are even more extreme, more alien, deadlier, than any you have encountered.

"Now the President has created the National Aeronautics and Space Administration and has charged it to bring together and direct all the various efforts towards space conquest. The time had come when a central command had to be set up to drive forward, and to overcome the lead in this space race demonstrated by our powerful competitor on the other side of the Pole.

"For this is a race, there is no doubt of it. It is entirely possible that whoever fully masters space flight first, whoever first establishes strong bases on other planets, will be able to enforce their viewpoint on all the other people of the world. We are proud of our own nation. We defend our own American way of life, and we are absolutely determined that it shall prevail. This is a race to conquer space, indeed, and the grand prize for the winner is not going to be some strange planet, but this one. The winner will win Earth.

"Bear that in mind. Never forget it, no matter what you do or how hard your task in the days and years to come. The Earth is the first prize."

"The Earth is the first prize," the colonel said.

The colonel paused dramatically, looked around again, searching each eye. The room was silent. The fellows in their varied uniforms were leaning forward as one, sharp, keen. Mike felt his own veins pulsing, and in the back of his mind a little voice whispered, "This is it, this is for real."

The colonel grasped the rostrum with both hands, spoke again.

"Just about the first thing that N.A.S.A. did was to set up this Space Task Group and charge it with organizing this project. The purpose is simply stated. We are going to begin the next important step in space flight. We are going to pick the men who will be the first to go up into the airless depths riding a rocket and return. Specifically we are going to launch a man into an orbit around the earth and bring him down again safely. Someone here is going to be that man; several of you will follow him. The first space fliers are sitting right here in this room."

The listeners stirred and Mike heard the soft hiss of long breaths coming out in hushed whistles.

The colonel nodded. "Yes, I have no doubt that among you are the men who are going to achieve what countless others in past years have dreamed of. You are fortunate in the years you picked to be born. You are the generation that's going to do it.

"But don't suppose the doing will be easy. It won't. It will be hard, it will be . . . deadly. You'll get no guarantees of life and fame. The records of the early days of aviation are dotted with the names of those who were killed trying. There is no reason to suppose that the task of putting up a manned satellite will not have as many martyrs.

"I hope you have all thought of that when you applied for this project. If you haven't, think of it during the next few days, and if you feel that you're not ready to give your life for this ride on a rocket, I want you to come to me and ask to be let out. Your request will be granted immediately, and there will be no mark on your record. Don't be ashamed of it. Consider it your duty; if you are unwilling to take the risks that this will involve, consider it a duty to withdraw.

"I am going to tell you something else now. The Space Task Group has not set up Project Quicksilver alone. There is a similar project in operation with identical aims, and it is known as Project Mercury. You may hear of this in the course of your training; you will hear a lot of it later on and wonder why you do not hear of your own project. This, too, is part of our planning.

"There is you see a difference of opinion on the right men for this task. One opinion holds that the astronauts should be picked from the ranks of experienced test pilots, men of great and invaluable experience in the flying of all kinds of strange new planes. Such men in general prove to be from ten to fifteen

41

years older than you chaps gathered here. We know that the reactions of youth are quicker than those of men even in their thirties, but it was felt that experience balanced out the odds.

"When we talked this over at N.A.S.A., we decided on two projects. One with the experienced men; that's Mercury. The other with the youngest group of newly qualified pilots possible, men who do not have fixed ideas or established flying habits, who would be at the very peak of their young powers; that's you, Project Quicksilver.

"Which group will succeed remains to be seen. I'm counting on you fellows. I hope you don't let me down."

He stopped again. The men twisted in their seats, looked around at each other with curious eyes. Things were getting down to brass tacks.

Colonel Drummond drew back a bit, surveying the group again. He spoke.

"We are going to pick seven men out of this group of candidates for Project Quicksilver. These will be the seven chosen for training as astronauts, and that's a new profession in the world. Astronaut. It means quite literally one who navigates among the stars. Not by the stars, but to the stars. It will be a mighty proud title in the centuries to come. Seven of you will be among the first ever to bear it.

"These seven are going to be picked after a complete series of examinations and tests. Some of these tests are simple medical examinations, such as you have had many times before in school and in your pilot training. We're doing them all over again, more carefully, more exactly. Some of these tests will determine how you would react and think in special conditions. Some of these tests will determine the limits of your ability to take punishment.

"They're not going to be easy. Don't think of these tests as competition which it would be a shame to fail. These tests are to find out exactly what you are now, what your ability is to the limit. You can't bone up for these tests. Again there's no shame involved in being eliminated. We want the seven who can stand up best under some pretty unnatural conditions. If you are not selected, consider it a favor—for it might well mean your life and a billion dollars worth of wasted effort and science if you were chosen by mistake.

"Now you are going to be here at the School of Aviation Medicine for about a week. During that time Dr. Holderlin and his assistants will put you through a whole series of careful physical examinations. Those are the first hurdles. After that, there'll be others, considerably more interesting—and even more exhausting.

"So, gentlemen, I am turning you over to Dr. Holderlin now. Good luck."

CHAPTER 6

SPACE MEDICINE

THE colonel sat down and the gray-haired civilian came to the stand. Mike studied him with interest. He had heard about the remarkable Dr. Hugo Holderlin before, and having been an ardent reader of magazine articles and stories dealing with efforts at space travel, he knew something about him.

Hugo Holderlin was one of the famous group of German scientists and engineers who had been brought over to the United States after the end of World War II and given the opportunity of resuming their researches this time on behalf of democracy. Mike knew that virtually all of these men had proved anxious about, and interested in, democracy—as men of learning they had served their country during wartime, but they had all known of the essential wrongness of the crazy ideas held by the Nazi leaders.

Holderlin had been a physician with the enemy air force. As such he had acquired a practical knowledge of the medical problems facing airmen.

In the years since he had come to America he had helped to develop the remarkable new branch of medicine that has come to be known as Space Medicine. Along with such men as Hubertus Strughold and Bruno Balke, he had conducted many researches designed to enable men to survive in the conditions of intense cold, airlessness, and weightlessness.

Holderlin looked over the crowd, examining it with apparently as much interest as it did him. He looked at Mike Mars, and Mike would have sworn he winked. He remembered how he had been singled out because of his unusual entrance. Well, did the doctor then have a sense of humor?

"Well, gentlemen," began the doctor with an obvious German accent, "so here we are. We are all waiting for you impatiently. We have our little needles and pins and test tubes—and some other little surprises waiting for you; and my young men, who are accustomed to guinea pigs, are anxious to begin finding out what makes you tick. However"—he looked at the clock on the back wall of the room—"I see it is getting late.

Half past eleven already. So maybe better you should have lunch and rest up a bit before we start.

"I have a card I want each of you to fill out first and then you can go and have lunch. Everybody come back here at half past one, please."

He asked a young Navy pilot who sat in the front row near him to hand out a stack of small white cards.

Mike took his. It was a standard business-machine form card, designed to go through a punching machine and carry all sorts of coded information. On it he wrote only his name, serial number, branch of service, date of birth, and birthplace. He looked at it as he finished. On it he knew the results of his various tests would be totaled up. In some spot, a hole would be punched at long last, and where that hole went would say in the language of a coding machine whether he would be on his way to the stars or on his way back to Nellis for assignment on earth.

A momentous bit of cardboard, indeed, he thought as he rose and made his way to the door. He handed it to the doctor, who was standing there as each man went out. Holderlin looked at the card, looked at him, as if to try to identify each man.

"Ah, yes," he said when he saw Mike, "the breathless young man who came last." He looked at Mike's card, read his name, "Aha!" he exclaimed. "I see why the colonel thought you had come all the way from the red planet. The initials on your helmet, they were not that at all, but just Michael A. R. Samson. Well," he looked at Mike, eyes twinkling, "we'll see whether you would like to be a Martian yourself, by and by."

Mike felt himself flush a little bit, but he grinned it off and found himself in the hall. At once Johnny Bluehawk and Marty Sherrod grabbed him, pumped his hand, and slapped his back. "You made it!" Johnny was elated. "How did you do it? When did you get your orders?"

Mike exchanged greetings, "I'll tell you about it at lunch. I'm starved. I haven't had breakfast yet, and I've got to find a place to bunk."

They went off to the cafeteria. The School of Aviation Medicine was a big, busy center. It combined the facilities of a clinic with those of a medical school. There were many earnest young student physicians going to and from classrooms and laboratories. The building was new and large and already bustling. As they went Johnny explained that they would all be bunking together in a dormitory in the school itself. They had spent the last night in quarters on the base, but from that day on they'd all be under supervision.

"I haven't got a thing," Mike said, "I'll have to draw some clothes until I can get my own stuff shipped from Nellis. I better remember to have my flying outfit sent back there, along with the plane I borrowed."

When they were seated at one of the tables and eating their lunch, Mike told them how he had found his lost orders in Harger's room. Marty and Johnny were both angry.

"Sounds to me," said Marty, "as if he had deliberately hidden them away. If you hadn't shown up, you'd have been crossed off this project."

The young Indian was even more emphatic. "He doesn't like you, Mike," he said. "I never thought he was a particularly friendly guy, but I never realized how much he really hates your guts until he said a few things while we were coming down here. I think Marty is right. I'll bet he lost your orders on purpose."

Mike chewed his sandwich thoughtfully. "I don't like to accuse anybody, fellows," he said. "Rod's a good flier, whatever you say, and I always figure he knows the tradition of the Air Force as well as we do. No, I don't want to think it was deliberate. I'm going to take the attitude he lost the papers by accident."

"But you better keep an eye on him pretty carefully from now on," said Marty, and Johnny nodded emphatically.

"I will," said Mike. "Though I don't see what he can do here. We have to try to keep ourselves from getting upset about this. If I know anything about medical tests, it could show up in our blood pressure. So let's calm down and keep cool. The best way to show Rod up would be to win out in this astronauts selection."

It was half past one soon enough. By that time, Mike had arranged for his replacement clothing and for the return of the plane. When all the fellows were back in the small assembly room, Dr. Holderlin called them to attention.

"We will divide you into several groups of a half dozen or so each, and you will be started on your tests in these groups for easy handling." An assistant came in, with a prepared list, and read off the names of each man present. Mike was pleased to find that he was in the same group with Johnny Bluehawk. Marty and Rod Harger were together in another group.

Mike's bunch got up and followed the white-coated young doctor who was to put them through their paces.

Most of the afternoon was taken up with a lengthy questionnaire: each man sat at the doctor's desk answering innumerable questions about his background. Did he ever have mumps, measles, whooping cough, all sorts of other illnesses? His parents and their illnesses? His grandparents, their relatives? When something was unknown, it was left blank and the young doctor explained that somehow an investigator would find out.

This was followed by exact measurements, by general examinations of the body, by withdrawal of blood and other specimens for analysis and laboratory testing. The afternoon ended with a series of X-ray studies, and even X-ray motion pictures of the beating heart to determine the presence of any unsuspected imperfections.

During the next two days the boys were subjected to more of the same thing, but in such exactness as they had not dreamed of. The examining doctors—Dr. Holderlin's enthusiastic assistants—spared them nothing in their efforts to ferret out the last secrets of their physical health.

The eye examinations alone lasted hours, with all manner of lights and minute and often painful measurements, such as those to determine the inner pressure on the eyes, dark and light shifts to determine their ability to adjust to night sight and to react to sudden glares, photography of the back of the eye.

Their hearing and ears were tested in just as minute fashion.

Mike did his best and hoped he heard right.

There was a session with earphones while Mike wrote down the words and numbers he heard—or thought he heard—under various difficult conditions. Several such tests were really tricky: he was asked to copy down things being said against backgrounds of different kinds of noises—thuds, screams, engine sounds, thunder, other people talking, and so on.

Mike did his best, and hoped he heard right. Sometimes he was afraid it was only guesswork to suppose what one person was saying when all around (in the record to which his earphones were plugged) were sounds like a boiler factory full of shrill people!

Talking about them at night, the fellows were often able to figure out what purpose these tests had in connection with space flight. After all, suppose a fellow was heading into orbit in a rocket ship and had to keep contact with the Earth several hundred miles below. The radio voice might be drowned in static; it might be weak and far away; there could be all sorts of outside noises. Maybe the rocket itself was rumbling and vibrating. It could mean a good deal if the men in charge knew that their pilot had the kind of hearing that could single out the one weak voice that counted.

The same applied to eyesight. If there was an accidental flare, an explosion, or even an unexpected glimpse at the unshielded sun, how quickly would the pilot get his normal vision back so that he could read the controls? Just a little thing like a slow adjustment could be enough to eliminate a man from the astronaut selection.

"I understand that tomorrow we're going to get some really tiring tests," Mike said as he sat on his bed in the dormitory which housed the entire group. He was talking to Johnny and Jack Lannigan, a young Navy flier, who was in his group and to whom he had taken a liking. Jack was a redhead, a strapping six-footer who had once played against Mike in high school basketball during an interschool competition. They had been amused to meet each other again in these unusual surroundings and the former athletic antagonism proved a good bond for friendship.

"Yeah," said Jack. "The doc wouldn't tell me exactly what. But he said we ought to catch up on our rest tonight." He looked at his watch. "It's only eight o'clock. I had been hoping to get into town tonight for a couple hours. Maybe have a soda, look the town over, get away from this hospital atmosphere."

Mike shook his head. "I'd love to, but I think we'd better

call it off for tonight. If the doc gave us a hint, we'd be smart to take it. Me, I'm going to hit the sack."

"Yeah," Jack said, and Johnny nodded, too, "guess so. But I see one guy who ain't going to give up so easy."

He indicated with his eyes across the aisle. Rod Harger was putting the final touches on his walking-out uniform; he brushed some imaginary lint from his shoulder, took down his blue garrison cap, ran an elbow over the silver eagle badge on its front, adjusted it over his pale straw-colored hair, and, glancing coldly over to where the three were sitting, strode confidently down the aisle and out the door.

Rod glanced coldly at them.

"I wonder where he's going, all dressed up," said Johnny. "No place good, I'm sure."

"So, more fool him," said Mike.

"I'd like to follow him and see," said Lannigan, looking after him. "That's one guy I can't get happy about."

But he didn't. If he had, and had made himself invisible enough to have kept within hearing distance of Rod, it might have been a most enlightening experience.

CHAPTER 7

THE HARGER PLAN

ROD Harger went into San Antonio and took a taxi to a large hotel in the center of the city. There he went directly to a certain room on an upper floor and knocked.

It was opened by a stocky, middle-aged man whose once blond hair showed silvery streaks of gray. He was a pale man with pale eyes and the kind of sharp bulldog wrinkles in his jaw which indicated a man accustomed to having his own way. Had anyone else been observing he would have noted a great resemblance between this man and his caller in Air Force blue.

"Hello, dad," said Rod to his father as he went into the hotel room of Rodney S. Harger, Sr. "I made it on time, but I can't stay long. I hear there's some strenuous tests coming tomorrow and I can't afford to lose out on sleep."

"O.K., son, I just wanted to see you. I'll make it brief. You ain't going to lose out, just don't you worry about it." The elder Harger gestured at the bed, and Rod sat down.

Drawing up a chair, his father looked at him in silence, then drew out a cigar, clipped the end, stuck it in his mouth, took out an expensive lighter, and lit up. Taking a puff or two, he allowed his thin lips to break briefly into the flicker of a smile.

"You'll do," he said. "We Hargers are tough stuff. You're going to be one of the astronauts, and you're going to be the one that gets up there first."

Rod shrugged. "I'd like to hope so. But as the colonel who briefed us said, you get no guarantees."

"Nuts to him," said his father coldly. "I'm giving you a guarantee. You just keep your health up and pass those tests. There's too much at stake that somebody like that colonel never thinks about. There's a fortune in it—and the kind of fame that'll keep you in velvet the rest of your life."

Rod looked at his father. He had a great respect for his opinion. He had tried hard to be as tough as his father, and he knew he still had a long way to go.

"Let me remind you, son," said his father, taking his cigar out of his mouth and jerking it around as if to emphasize his

"We Hargers are tough stuff," Harger, Sr., said.

remarks, "that the first man up in space is going to have as much fame as Columbus, especially the first to set foot on the moon. The book sales, magazine stories, television and radio rights alone would make him a mint. I aim to see that the dough that's in all that doesn't go to waste. That first man could name his own salary in a dozen big companies that would want his name for promotion. If he's smart enough to get out of uniform at the right time, he's made."

Rod looked down at his uniform. "I choose the Air Force because I like flying. I like the life in the service."

His father sneered. "You'll get over that. Why, heck, you can buy a dozen airplanes later. Don't you want to be famous and rich? Don't you like the idea of the name of Rodney S. Harger being known for hundreds of years to come, with statues and places named after you and so on?"

Rod smiled thinly. He leaned forward slightly himself. "Now you're talking. I have always dreamed of that kind of thing."

His father nodded. "We see eye to eye. Rodney S. Harger.

That's us, both of us. There's plenty in it for me, too. So forget this service stuff. We're in a fight and we're going to fight hard—and dirty, too. Let the others be 'officers and gentlemen'—we mean business. Now listen . . ."

He leaned over. "You made this group of candidates, now all you got to do is to be among the top seven. The way we guarantee that is by seeing that things happen to the fellows who look like they may be as good as you or better. You

Jack Lannigan

already showed some sense when you sidetracked this Mike Mars' orders. Too bad it didn't work out. But next time it will.

"I've hired a man who's going to help you—from the outside. He's one of the G.I.'s I knew when I was making my

52

pile during the war in the black market. Sure, I was in a uniform, too, but while the other G.I.'s were fighting, I was getting my hands on the means of making a fortune. You've lived pretty well in your young life—remember, it took some pretty dirty work on my part to fix it up that way. I expect you to do your share."

Rod nodded. His father went on. "Now this fellow used to be an aviator, a jet pilot even. He got tossed out of the service for a few things I don't mention and he's real interested in getting even. He won't stop at anything. He's going to be hanging around wherever you fellows are, and every time he gets the chance to put some of your rivals out of the running he's going to do it. Little things, maybe, like a little accident with a car; maybe something will drop on them when they are passing under it; maybe they'll get ptomaine poisoning when they eat the wrong things; maybe they'll just be delayed in one way or another.

"You see, the whole idea is that just any little accident, a broken leg, getting lost somewhere, could be enough to eliminate them from these tests. So suppose you give me a list of the fellows you think my man can get to work on. We'll start by listing this Mike Mars who managed to get to be team leader instead of you at Nellis."

He took out a little notebook and put down the half dozen names Rod gave him. "O.K.," he said, "you just do your work, keep your nose out of trouble, and let us do the rest."

He stood up and Rod got up, too. His father slapped him on the back and showed him to the door. Rod went back to the base, and as he went his mind was full of dreams about a great hero who had returned from the moon to find the world at his feet. Not for one instant did the thought of patriotism enter his dream, for the hero was himself; and standing behind him, modestly in the shadows, was his father.

The tests next day were indeed strenuous. So were the problems the would-be astronauts faced the remaining days at the school. It would be hard to outline each and all of them, for in themselves they might not be too interesting, but there were some that none of the fellows who participated ever forgot.

The most painful was a series of internal examinations, wherein probes were directed into various parts of the body. In one instance a tube had to be swallowed that reached down to the stomach to take up samples of the digestive juices. In other instances delicate little needles were inserted into the scalp and flesh of the body to register the electrical charges of the nerves and to determine what differences were to be noted when the man to be tested was given certain stimuli.

Mike found it at first ticklish, then painful, finally rather startling. With a half dozen little clamps and points jutting into him like a pincushion, and with large meters watched by intent observers, he had to respond to various stimulations. Then, without his knowledge, little electric shocks were sent into him through these needles to determine the automatic responses of various muscles and nerves. Sometimes the reaction felt cold, sometimes it was like a sting of fire; at other moments that particular part of his body would become numb.

None of the men liked this sort of thing, but each recognized the need for such studies. Nothing, literally nothing, could be overlooked.

Then there was the afternoon spent on the ergometer. This was a device exactly like a bicycle, except that it was stationary. You sat on the saddle and pedaled away and it registered how much energy you were putting into it. Mike supposed it could also tell how far you presumably were cycling, but they didn't bother to tell him that.

This would have been easy enough, save for the additional burdens they put on the men. Mike found that pedaling this bike-contraption while wearing an oxygen mask and having various clamps attached to his body to register his heartbeats and blood pressure was not so pleasant. It got rapidly harder as they added resistance to the pedals to simulate an increase in weight.

Mike pedaled away, feeling himself steadily growing wearier as he forced the pedals down with the same amount of effort as it would take to cycle not only himself but also a couple of other men sitting on his shoulders. He knew the reason for this test—it was one means of demonstrating his capacity for carrying hard loads and for determining just how much oxygen his lungs would use during an ordeal as well as how strong his heart was.

He was tired clear through when he was done with this, but he noted to himself as he made his way to rest before his next workout that the other men in his group weren't any fresher. Only the doctors could tell who had worked the hardest for the same results—and they wouldn't reveal that until the final summing up.

Another series of tests with the oxygen masks involved various sorts of exercises—walking, running, jumping.

On another morning a team from the Los Alamos Laboratories arrived and tested each man for his natural bodily radiation count. After that, other tests determined the difference in weight of each man while entirely under water as against his weight in air. Nothing was overlooked.

By the end of the seventh day the men felt as if they had been subjected to just about every fiendish thing that had ever been dreamed up. They had given up ideas of going into town for a night off. They were content to flop into bed at the end of their day and get the rest.

Dr. Holderlin managed to be around at least part of the time during all these many tests. He had a wry sort of humor and the kind of personality that made the men feel that their troubles would not be wasted.

He remembered Mike, as he seemed to have a knack for remembering each man. He would come up to Mike, slap him on the back, and say something like, "How you feel now, boy? So

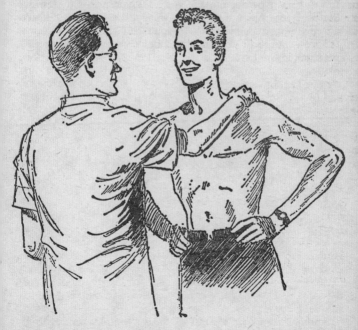

"How you feel now, boy?"

55

full of holes like craters yet, you must be Mike Moon, not Mike Mars any more, eh?"

"Oh, well, sir," Mike answered on that occasion, "the moon first, you know."

The doctor looked at the progress chart his assistant was working on. "That's right, that's right. You just keep the spirits up, you get there, by golly. But you wait and see what we got in store for you next."

But, at the end of that seventh day, Dr. Holderlin and Colonel Drummond came around unexpectedly to the dormitory just before lights out. They stood just inside the door and looked over the men.

When the fellows fell silent and looked back at them, the two men smiled. The colonel spoke, "I'm told you made a good showing, men. There will be a general session tomorrow at eight. Get your duffel together, and pack your belongings. Bring them along; we'll be pulling out."

The doctor beamed. "Ja," he said, "we've done all we can to you here. Now for most of you a little excursion tomorrow. Some of you may not be getting enough fresh air in this nice air-conditioned building. Well, soon enough you get plenty fresh air. So go to sleep now and don't worry. No more pins get stuck in you here."

CHAPTER 8

TWO MILES NEARER THE MOON

MIKE slept like a log the last night at the School of Aviation Medicine. There was a feeling of having passed the first set of hurdles. He had an idea that anything that could come after wouldn't be quite so deliberately painful as some of the things they had gone through.

As far as he could tell, nothing had gone amiss with him or his friends. Of course, they couldn't be certain, for no information had been released as to how well or how poorly anyone might have done. But it was possible by comparing his own feelings with the experiences of the others to assume that there was nothing to be discouraged about in his showing.

Johnny and Marty agreed that this had not been so bad after all. So the next day found them all in quite good spirits. There was a lot of bantering and kidding around as they arose early and began packing their stuff. Slinging their kit bags over their shoulders they legged it down to the cafeteria and the whole bunch made it the lightest-hearted eating session of the week.

Outside it was a typical South Texas day—hot, cloudless, and dry. Most of the fellows had gotten to know each other, and the rivalry that would ordinarily have existed between the Air Force boys and the Navy boys had managed to dissipate itself in a certain new camaraderie of Project Quicksilver. "Companions in misery," as Marty Sherrod called it.

Rod Harger retained a certain aloofness from the others, but not enough to make himself noticeably conspicuous. He was sure he had come through all right, for he had always kept himself in good physical condition. He wondered when his father's "friend" would begin to put in some work. He didn't have long to wait.

They gathered in the same room as before. The colonel and Dr. Holderlin turned up on time. The colonel spoke briefly, congratulating them on completing their tests. "There are now twenty-four in our group; two of our applicants have reconsidered during the past week. You are a remarkably healthy group of men, and I can say that the doctors will have a hard time deciding between you. Now originally we had planned to transfer you to your next series of tests, which were to be in Dayton, Ohio. However, the facilities there turn out to be in use for the candidates of Project Mercury, so instead we have something else for you for this next week." He turned to the doctor who took the stand.

"You are lucky, maybe, because we are now going to see some nice scenery and have maybe a little vacation. For you maybe not a vacation but another workout, but for me and the colonel, maybe we get some loafing and maybe fishing out of it. We are going by plane right away this morning to a nice mountain spot in Colorado. You'll do a little hiking, a little mountain, climbing, a little track exercises, heh? Sounds good, *nicht wahr?* So let's go, gentlemen."

He went out the door and the men filed out after him, giving each other rather startled glances. Mike fell in with Johnny as they picked up their bags and started down the hall with the others. "I don't like his cheerful smile. There must be a catch to it."

The young Cheyenne nodded. "By now, you know that for a fact. Still, Colorado mountains sound good. No matter what it is it'll be better than this place for me. It's not too far from my home grounds up in Montana.

They left by the main entrance of the school and waited around outside. As they stood there, waiting for transportation to the airfield, Mike noticed a black civilian car parked by the sidewalk about a block away. He could see that its engine was running, for he saw a faint vapor of exhaust. He didn't pay it any further attention, but Rod Harger did. Rod's eyes narrowed, and he picked up his bag and moved to the front of the crowd.

The blue bus arrived from the motor pool and the men started to climb in. Mike and Johnny were near the end of the line waiting to get in when Mike noticed that the strange car had started. It was moving away from the curb now, and heading in their direction. He looked down, picked up his bag, and started to the bus entrance.

Suddenly he heard the sound of an engine at full roar. He turned his head and saw that the black car, apparently out of control, had swerved and was tearing straight for the sidewalk in front of the School of Aviation Medicine. "Look out!" Mike yelled and tried to push the fellows in front of him out of the way.

The young men saw the car rushing at them, almost on top

"Look out!" Mike yelled.

of them. Its horn was honking now, rather belatedly, Mike thought afterwards. Most of the fellows were already in the bus. The colonel was standing by the door and he had started to yell.

The wild car careened up on the sidewalk. Two fellows on the end of the line jumped aside and escaped injury by a matter of inches. But one man was not so lucky. There was a slight soft bump and Mike saw someone thrown off his feet and rolling against the building.

The car swerved violently, avoided crashing into the front of the building, and came to a halt a couple of dozen feet away, its fenders scraping the stone wall.

There was a concerted rush by everyone for the young man who lay groaning on the sidewalk. Mike, having dropped his bag, was among them. When he reached the youth there were already others alertly bending over him. He looked around for the offending car.

It stood there, its engine silent, and there was no sign of anyone in it. Mike turned away from the growing crowd and ran over to the car. Perhaps, he thought, the driver is unconscious or dead.

But when he reached it, there was no one inside. Quickly he glanced ahead, and thought he saw a man in olive technician's coveralls go around the corner of the building.

He ran down to the corner, but when he got there, there was no one in sight. He walked back to the group around the injured man. "Very strange," he said to Marty Sherrod, who had come after him to look over the wild car. "No sign of the driver. He must have run away to avoid taking the consequences. It looked almost deliberate."

Marty nodded his head. "It was wild, real wild. Lucky only one man was hurt. He could have gotten several of us."

The injury could have been worse. The man who had been struck, a likable young fellow who had been among those who had come down from Nellis, had a badly scraped arm and what looked like a broken ankle, not to mention severe bruises. "He'll recover," said Dr. Holderlin, rising to his feet after examining the injuries, "but not in time to take any more part in these tests. I'm sorry for him, because he looked like a good candidate. But he'll have to be eliminated."

As they finished filing into the bus, Mike looked back and saw attendants carrying the injured boy back on a stretcher. It seemed to him that the pain in the young pilot's face did not come from his injuries but from the bitter disappointment of having to be left behind. It put a damper on everyone's spirits.

Not until they were on the big Air Force transport, a four-engined Superconstellation, and air-bound for Colorado did they begin to shrug off their depression and regain some of the good humor with which the morning had started.

The rest of the trip was comparatively uneventful: several hours in the air, with the men reclining in the comfortable seats, sometimes snoozing, reading magazines, shooting the breeze, or just looking out the windows watching the landscape roll by—so much easier than having to pilot a rip-roaring jet thunderbolt yourself. They put down at Denver, changed to another big bus, and drove several more hours up into the high mountains to the west of the Mile High City.

When finally they tumbled out of their seats and stood around, it was already late afternoon. The scenery was indeed beautiful. All around them rose the peaks of great mountains, the Mount Evans Range, as the colonel explained. A lovely blue lake could be seen nearby among the trees. The sky was clear and cloudless; the air was cold and nippy.

"So this is the place the doctor is going to get some fishing done, eh?" Mike said. Johnny nodded.

"It looks terrific. Just the place to spend a vacation, too. Only something tells me it's not going to be very much of a holiday for us," his bronzed friend added.

"I found out where we are," said Jack Lannigan, coming up. "This is called Echo Lake, and that big peak over there, beyond it, that's Mount Evans. I think I know what the catch is."

"What is it?" Johnny and Mike asked as one.

The Navy pilot inhaled and exhaled slowly. "This place is two miles high, that's all. Ever been two miles up in the air without an airplane? Well, you are now."

"Hmmm," Mike exhaled slowly himself as he looked around at the deceptively lovely landscape. "Two miles nearer the moon anyway."

Some of them just watched the landscape.

CHAPTER 9

THE DEEP BREATHERS

"THE amount of work we do depends on the amount of oxygen we breathe, because oxygen is the element in the air that we need to keep our bodies operating, our minds working, and life itself going. At normal air levels, such as at sea level or near it, where most of the world's cities and people live, we all know how much we can do, what is normal for breathing and eating and sleeping.

"Now the higher up we go, the thinner the air. The thinner the air, the less oxygen in it. This means that our lungs have to work harder and harder to bring the same amount of oxygen we would need down where the air pressure is more what we're built for. This applies in particular to the heart, which, as you know, pumps the oxygen from our lungs to our muscles and brain and the other organs of our body. The higher up, the thinner the air, and the harder and faster the heart must beat just to keep our bodies going."

The colonel paused, looked around at the group of serious young fellows seated around on the ground listening to him. The morning sun was still low in the sky, yet the Project Quicksilver candidates had already had breakfast and now, dressed in fatigue clothes, sweatshirts, and work shoes, were being briefed on the plans for this new experience.

Mike Mars had noticed the basketball courts near the lake and had mentioned something to Johnny and the other fellows about making up a game if they had time after their workout. But he had also noticed the long metal building tucked away part way up the mountain beyond the lake. He recognized it as a pressure chamber laboratory—for he had already had some experience in one during his early training.

"As pilots you already understand this. That is why you wear oxygen masks when flying at altitudes over 25,000 feet. Otherwise the lack of sufficient oxygen in the thinner air at that level and higher would cause you to become unconscious. Your body would not be able to pump enough blood to your brain to make it possible to retain consciousness.

"Now we have brought you up here to test your individual

ability to adjust to less oxygen without masks. Here, where we are two miles up, you will not lose consciousness, but your hearts and lungs will have to pump much harder to do the same amount of work. You are going to go through a series of exercises—running, jumping, weight-lifting—just as you might back at sea level. You're going to find yourself getting tired very much more quickly. You are going to take a tough hike through the mountains in a couple days, and that, too, will be a test. First, however, Doctor Holderlin is going to take all of you through a test in the pressure chamber."

The men got to their feet, formed into a column of twos, and followed him along the path up the mountainside to the long tubular metal structure, which looked like a long large sewer pipe on its side, and had a door on one side and a small building on the other. Mike knew there would be windows from that building and that the persons controlling the test would direct the withdrawal of air from that end.

Already on even this short hike, Mike noticed that he was breathing hard. It was as if he had just made a fast walk of several miles, yet he couldn't have walked more than half a mile. Indeed, you did not notice the thinness of the air, except as it made itself known by your beating heart and your straining lungs.

The fellows were allowed to rest for a few minutes until they were breathing normally again. Then they filed into the chamber and took seats on opposite sides of the long metal room inside. Mike saw the colonel and the doctor outside through the glass in the little room. The doctor picked up a microphone. His voice boomed overhead through a little speaker.

"We are going to bring you all up to about 30,000 feet level, according to the air pressure available there. What is going to happen is that you are going to have difficulty keeping conscious. But we want you to try very hard. Just sit still and breathe normally. O.K.?"

The fellows nodded. There was a slight click and a faint hissing noise was heard. Mike looked across the chamber at the fellows sitting there. Rod Harger was confident and cool, his eyes staring at the floor. Johnny Bluehawk, just opposite Mike, winked and smiled. Marty Sherrod had his hands folded, just waiting.

"At 13,000," said the voice of the colonel. That would be the reading for the air pressure level. Then "14,000" and, shortly after, the next thousand level.

So far, Mike was having no difficulty. But the numbers climbed slowly. At 22,000 he began to feel a little uncomfortable, noticed his lungs were working hard and his heart beginning to pound a little. The other men began to squirm uneasily. "At 23,000," said the colonel's voice, and one of the men began to sigh uneasily. Mike kept calm, breathed deeply, held on.

But by the time he heard the colonel say "25,000," Mike felt he was close to the end. Already he noticed that about two thirds of the men were slumped back, lungs pounding, but apparently asleep. Marty was out; Rod was hanging on, but looking sick. Johnny was wavering, his head nodding, his face strained. Mike heard "25,500" called out after what seemed an endless wait. He felt himself getting dizzy; for an instant he thought the lights had blinked.

He slipped down in his seat, his heart thundering as if it would burst. He gritted his teeth. His sight was graying out; things were getting vague. He saw Rod and Marty and even Johnny slumped down, and finally he swayed and gave way to black unconsciousness.

Suddenly he woke again. All around him the men were shaking their heads, looking at each other brightly as if to say, "What happened?" The pressure was normal, and his heart was no longer banging away. The rubber-edged door at the end swung open. Dr. Holderlin stuck his head in. "Everybody have a little nap? O.K., now we get some exercise, *ja?*"

The young pilots filed out. Mike passed the doctor and the colonel and heard the German exclaim, "You know, that was very good. A little better than normal even at the beginning. These are a fine group, *ja.* They adjust well. We see what happens at the end of the week."

They spent the rest of the day just as had been predicted. There were a series of track events which, had they taken place at a high school meet, would have been fun, but which proved to be very exhausting. A mere race of a hundred yards left the runners gasping like fish out of water.

By the end of the long day—and it was hot when the sun was high—the men were thoroughly worn out. As they marched back to their evening meal and bed, Mike shook his head as they passed the basketball courts. "Not tonight," he said to Johnny, who merely gave a tired laugh.

After supper that first night, they had a brief chance to loll around before hitting the blankets. The sunset was spectacular in those mountains. As the sun was setting there came a hum-

Mike felt himself getting dizzy.

A small blue plane came over the mountains.

ming noise, and a small blue airplane came over the mountains. The men looked. It was a private plane, a Cessna. It passed over the field, swung around, circled as if to give its passenger a chance to look the men over. Then it flew away, back the way it had come.

Mike listened to its hum on the clear air. It seemed to stop rather suddenly. "You know," he remarked to Jack Lannigan, who was nearest, "it sounds to me like that plane set down not too far from here. Just over the mountain somewhere."

Jack nodded. "It sounded that way. Some rubberneck from Denver way."

Rod Harger also had looked after the disappearing plane. He smiled to himself. Dad was on the job, he thought.

During the next few days, the men went through an increasing series of hikes and exercises. Strangely enough, they found themselves doing better and better. On the afternoon of the third day, it was the doctor himself who organized a couple of basketball games, dividing the men up into teams.

Mike had a good workout then. It was fun and the fact that Rod was on the opposing team made it even more exciting. There were a couple of instances when it seemed to him that Rod had deliberately tried to trip him, knee him, or shove him, but Mike was too good a player for that. He evaded Rod's efforts and laughed to himself when Lannigan, on Mike's team, did slam unexpectedly into Rod and sent that chunky young man sprawling.

But playing basketball at a two-mile high level was plenty tiresome, and the fellows slept deeply that night.

The fifth day was a special. They were organized into two hiking teams and were going to climb the side of Mount Evans. It would be an all-day hike, and each man carried a light pack with him. The mountain was 14,000 feet high, although they were already up ten of those fourteen thousand. It was not too impossible a mountain; there were trails and a few tight squeezes, but the trip turned out to be one that did not involve very special mountaineering equipment.

The two teams, taking different routes, met on top early in the afternoon. They were exhausted but in good spirits. After a half hour of loafing around on top, and good appetites for the food they had packed, the climb down began.

Coming down they were often in shade as the sun began to descend in the sky. Each team came down by the route the other team had used in ascending, and so it was new all the way.

Mike and Johnny were at the end of the line as they made their way along the narrow rocky paths with the towering sides over them and long dangerous rocky drops falling away at their feet. Just ahead of Mike was Marty Sherrod, picking his way along. The team had stretched out and the next man

Marty had lost his balance.

ahead of Marty was already about twenty yards away, and often out of sight.

The rest of the men had already made their way around a sharp curve and down through a narrow pass when the three men, the last ones, came along an open path not more than a couple of feet wide. Below was a steep drop of broken rock. The scene was wide and they could see the slope of another mountain in the Evans Range close by, perhaps a few hundred yards away.

Mike looked at it as they trekked. All were tired, for the going was tricky here and they were all now slightly breathless. He thought he saw something flash on the opposite mountain. "See that?" he called to Johnny, who was bringing up the rear.

The Indian looked, squinted. "Somebody over there," he said. "Maybe a hunter."

As he looked there was a blink of yellow-red like a spark. Something *spanged* off the rock over their heads.

"Hey!" cried Mike. "We're being shot at!"

There was another spark, a whistling echo. Suddenly, in front of Mike, Marty Sherrod jumped, gave a yell, and fell to his knees. Mike dashed to him, but before he could reach him, Marty had lost his balance, slid over the edge.

Another nasty *spang,* and a chip of rock just over Mike's head was gouged out of the cliffside.

CHAPTER 10

RUNNER IN THE DARKNESS

"GET down!" Mike yelled and fell flat on the narrow ledge of rock. Johnny had done the same as fast as Mike had. Another bullet chipped a piece of rock from a point a few feet above their heads.

Mike edged over to the side and looked down. The mountainside fell away sharply below them, but it was not a straight-up-and-down cliffside. It was rather a very steep and rocky incline, with here and there a small bush forcing its way out of cracks between the chunks and strips of rock.

Marty had rolled down about twenty feet and was now lodged against a couple of the stumpy bushes on a small level of outthrust rock. He wasn't moving; he was just lying there in an odd and twisted position. "Think he's dead?" whispered Johnny, who had poked his head over for a look, too.

"We'll have to go down. He may be just unconscious. Could have struck his head against a rock on the way down," Mike said slowly. "You didn't see where he was hit?"

"Huh-uh," said Johnny. "Where's the rest of the squad? Didn't anybody hear those shots?"

Mike looked back. "The mountainside must have cut off the noise. I hope they find out we're not with them." He hesitated. "Look, Johnny, you see if you can catch up to them, get some help. I'm going to go down there and see how he is."

Johnny protested that he was the one to go down, but another shot whistling low over their heads showed them that this was no time to argue. So Johnny started off, crawling on hands and knees until he could get out of sight of the gunner and run after the rest of the party. It would be slow going.

Meanwhile, Mike shucked off his pack and slipped carefully over the side. He began to make his way down the steep slope, holding on to brush and bits of rock. There was another *spang*, and a chunk bit out of the side just over his head. He was a sitting pigeon in this position, but he couldn't let that bother him. Marty's life was at stake and it was already clear that the hidden marksman was a little too far away to be very

The sniper shot off several more bullets.

exact in his shots. So Mike ignored the several bullets that pinged and caromed around him, and crawled down foot by foot.

Halfway to Marty's position, the shooting stopped. Mike cautiously turned his head and, looking across to the opposing mountainside, saw that the spot where the shooter must have been concealed was now cut off from view by a formation of rock on that other slope. This accounted for the lack of further bullets into Marty's helplessly exposed body.

He made the rest of the way down a little faster, his hands bruised and his shins scratched from the rough side. Digging a foot into some loose gravel for care, he swung his other foot onto the same little ledge Marty rested upon. He was able to reach his friend.

Marty was alive, but knocked out. There was a bruise on his forehead, where he had struck something while falling. There was a blotch of blood on one pants leg, and Mike realized that the marksman had scored a shot there.

"How is he?" came a voice from above. It was Johnny. Mike looked up, explained the wound. Johnny called down, "I couldn't find anyone . . . they've gone too far. I can't leave you alone up here."

Without further comment he, too, edged over and started down. There was one more *spang* from the rifleman—which missed—and in a short while Johnny was alongside Mike, hanging on cautiously.

The two friends conferred. Obviously they couldn't take Marty back up to the ledge. Looking down, they saw a fairly wide level section another twenty or thirty feet below them. "If we can get him down there," Mike said, "we can have enough room to stop his bleeding and keep him from falling more while one of us gets help."

They talked it over, and at last worked out a desperate tactic. Removing their belts and using Marty's shoulder pack for additional bindings, they worked the unconscious pilot onto Johnny's back and tied him there. Then, with Mike going first and testing the footgrips, and helping Johnny by bolstering him when possible, the young Indian made the descent safely.

Once on the wide level, they cut open the material of Marty's trousers, found the bullet wound. Plugging it with a clean handkerchief, they fashioned a simple tourniquet with a belt and stick. Then they took stock of their situation.

It was afternoon. In a little while the sun would be setting and the evening chill coming. One of them would have to stay there with the unconscious man, the other would have to try to make his way back to the camp at Echo Lake to get help.

"You carried him down the ledge, and that was pretty hard. So I'll go on to the camp and get the help," said Mike. Johnny tried to argue with him, but Mike pointed out that staying there was plenty hard and dangerous. If possible, he said, Johnny should make a fire as the sun went down. In that way they could be located, and also could keep warm. Marty had matches in his pocket and there was enough dry brush around to help.

Mike glanced around. It wouldn't be possible to climb back up the steep side to the original path—besides, who knew whether the rifleman was still waiting? So he would go down the slope again and work his way back to camp by dead reckoning.

He set out, slipping, sliding, and tumbling. Sometimes he could walk a few yards, other times it was catch-as-catch-can. He realized now how tired he was. Not only had they just had a hard day's mountain climb, but this extra burden, which he had not noticed during the emergency, was now also telling. His heart was pounding and he found himself very breathless. The atmosphere, he thought. You can't ignore it altogether.

He had to pause and rest frequently. He was in shade now, as the sun was sinking beyond the mountaintops, and a chill was already in the air. He pushed on, guiding himself by the glow of the sunlight on the western peaks and by his own reckoning as to where the road and lake should be.

It was dark when he finally found himself on level valley ground. He was weary and his clothes were torn and his hands bruised and sore. He stumbled on, forcing his legs to perform, deliberately breathing deeply and fast to keep his blood supply up, to keep himself warm. He tried to close his mind to his bone-tired condition; he refused to think of anything but the camp ahead and his two comrades crouched on the mountainside.

In the darkness he could not see familiar signs, but he felt sure he would be coming out on something soon. He wanted nothing more than to lie down and rest awhile, but he refused to give in. As he trudged along, he recalled a little poem he had made up when he was a boy, a poem he'd memorized and recited for his own amusement and to express his ambition. It was a variation on an old nursery rhyme, and it went this way:

Michael Mars is my name.
America's my nation.
Space-flying is my game
And Mars my destination!

It was while he was mumbling this little ditty for the ump-teenth time that he finally saw the lights of the buildings at Echo Lake. He hastened his steps.

Not long after, he was sitting in Dr. Holderlin's improvised office and telling his story to the doctor, the colonel, and as many of the pilots as managed to squeeze themselves in.

Now that Mike had told his story, the problem was more easily solved. A phone call to the nearest Air Force base brought a pair of helicopters buzzing overhead within an hour. Mike and the doctor climbed aboard the leader, and the two whirlybirds took off and headed out for the mountainside.

They searched the darkness below as they went, and it seemed just a couple of minutes before they spotted a tiny flicker of flame down in the darkness. With their searchlights going, the two helicopters came down, poised over the slope, and in no time Marty had been brought aboard in a sling with Johnny, hungry and chilled despite the fire, with him.

Of the rifleman there was no sign. It was obvious that who-ever it was had cleared out of the neighborhood.

The next day men of Air Force Intelligence flew in and combed the region for the unseen foe. They found where he had hidden on the ledge; they found a small camp where he must have stayed while waiting his chance. There was a level meadow and they saw the wheel-marks of a small plane on it.

"The search isn't over," said one of these men as they re-ported late the next day to the colonel. "We're going to check on all the private planes in this neighborhood. But it may take many days. Meanwhile you'd better go ahead with your program."

Marty had been removed to a Denver hospital and eliminated from becoming an astronaut. But he would regain the use of his leg without any permanent injury, thanks to Mike's and Johnny's actions.

"I think all you men realize now that we're in a real race," said the colonel as he briefed the men of Project Quicksilver the morning of their last day. "We don't know yet what was behind this vicious attack, but it was clearly a life-and-death matter to the snipers. It is a life-and-death matter to our country to win this race into space, and you all know now

The helicopter poised over the slope.

that other forces inside and maybe outside our country realize this. For you men, the way to fight this, to fight for your country's new space frontier, is to keep calm, to work at your tests, to keep your health and a level head. That's how to beat them. Let them play dirty, if they have to.

"You fellows play it straight. Remember now that these tests are not just a series of games, of simple endurance contests. The title of astronaut isn't just a ticket to fame and glory; it's a tough assignment. It's the firing line of space, the forward trenches in the biggest and deadliest frontier man ever faced."

Jack Lannigan was sitting on his cot when Mike and Johnny, bone-tired, were readying for sleep that night. And as they were undressing, he personally congratulated them—for he had grown to be a good friend of theirs, in spite of the rivalry between the Navy and Air Force boys in their group. Looking around, reassuring himself that no one else was within hearing, he leaned over and said:

"You fellows almost got dropped from the Project when you failed to show up. The colonel was very angry. I guess you've been too busy to wonder why we never sent out a searching party after you."

Mike untied his shoes, rubbed his aching feet. He looked up sharply. "That's right, now that you mention it. How come?"

Lannigan shook his close-cropped red hair. "Someone told the colonel you fellows had taken a short cut and got in ahead of us. Said he saw three fellows, looking like you, take a hitch with some airmen into the village for the evening."

Mike and Johnny sucked in their breath. "Who said that?" the Cheyenne asked.

"Harger," said the young Navy pilot.

Mike shook his head. "I guess he saw some other three fellows and made a mistake."

Johnny gave a short grunt. "A mistake? That's what he'll say if you ask him, but I wonder."

"Still," Mike said as he climbed into bed, "Rod's a darned good flier and one of the best in these tests, far as I can tell. Rather give him the benefit of the doubt."

As Johnny prepared to hit the sack, he caught Lannigan's eye. The two men shook their heads silently in agreement.

The last event at Echo Lake was exactly like the first. It was the pressure chamber and the TUC test, which was what it was called. That meant "time of useful consciousness"—the length of time a man could keep going intelligently at a point of low oxygen intake. This time there was a difference.

"Even one week at a high altitude can show up differing abilities to adjust," said Dr. Holderlin as the men took their seats in the chamber. "You will see, they will all have built up more ability to use their lungs and hearts to better advantage from just staying and working up here."

It was so. The first of the men to lose consciousness blacked out at 26,500 feet this time. Mike himself was among the last to weaken and fall into stupor—and he heard the doctor call 32,000 feet then.

CHAPTER 11

THE SILENCE OF OUTER SPACE

HE WAS in total darkness. Straining his eyes as much as he could, Mike could see nothing. All around him not so much as the faintest ray of light penetrated. This was darkness, beyond even the darkness of outer space, for that was lit by a million million stars. This was the sort of darkness that he might find exploring an airless cavern deep beneath the lunar crust.

It was silent. Straining his ears as much as he could, he could hear nothing. Sensitive eardrums, straining, could bring him the illusion of hearing his own heartbeat, of hearing the pulsing of blood in the tiny vessels of his ears. But no outside sound broke the quiet. This was as quiet as an airless cavern on the moon, as quiet as the cabin of a spaceship drifting endlessly between the planets.

For a while Mike sat and absorbed the curiousness of it all. Never in his life had he ever been in such total isolation. Even alone at home as a small boy, as had happened once or twice, he had never been so alone. There were always the faint noises of a settling house, of water in pipes, of tiny things, mice or insects somewhere, and, of course, noises from the street— distant but there. Only in outer space would there be such silence . . . out there between the worlds where no air moved, no life fluttered, no engine purred.

This was what it might be like to be a space flier. It was discomforting there could be no doubt. He squirmed, looked again hard, hunting for something to focus his eyes on, but there was nothing in the blackness and nothing to hear.

He smiled to himself suddenly, thought of saying something aloud just to hear a voice. His smile broke off. Surely that would count against him. This was an endurance test. Very well, let's compose ourselves, let's put our mind to work and in that way keep calm. Let there be no light, let there be no sound. A strong mind in a healthy body could endure it. We'll fool them.

First, who are we?

Well, we're Michael Alfred Robert Samson, known as Mike

Only in outer space would there be such silence.

Mars, and we're a newly commissioned pilot in the Air Force. We're being tested for ability to endure in space.

Second, where are we?

In outer space? In a cavern of the moon? No, not at all, despite the resemblance. We're in Dayton, Ohio. We're at the Wright-Patterson Air Force Base, along with the rest of the astronaut cadets. To be exact, we are at the Wright Air Development Center Aeromedical Laboratories, and we are all undergoing a series of endurance tests.

As Dr. Holderlin explained yesterday, when we were flown in from Colorado, these will be the last series of the tests and in some ways the most significant. We are going to be checked very carefully, very exactly for our ability to hold up under the kind of strain we may run into in space.

This is one of those tests. It's the isolation test. I've got to sit here until the test is over. They said it would take three hours of doing nothing here in this soundless, lightless room. How long is three hours? How long have I been here already?

I don't know, he thought to himself. There might be a way to figure out time by counting my heartbeats, about seventy to a minute would be average. But will they be average? If I can get a little panicky, the count will go up. If I fall asleep, it will go down. Better not—besides, it might put me to sleep. That would be a bad mark against me.

If I were out in space like this, going to sleep might be the death of me. So I've got to stay awake, just sit here and think.

Besides, they know what my heartbeat is. They have a clamp on my chest, a count on my blood pressure, a gauge on my temperature. They are measuring the number of breaths I take a minute. They'll know when I'm getting panicky. So keep calm, keep cool. Just think.

Never thought it would be so difficult just to do nothing.

Let's think about something else than this dark place. I'll think about Johnny Bluehawk, my best friend. He's a nice guy to know. He's quiet and calm, and the kind of fellow who'd stand by a man through thick and thin. Out where Johnny comes from the cowboys have a way of saying it. What's that phrase? Oh, yes. "He's a man to ride the river with."

Johnny must have had a hard life. He doesn't talk much about it, but I can tell. He's got iron in him. He had to have. The Northern Cheyenne Indians aren't rich ones. They're dirt poor, I understand. They're a proud people with a proud history. Plains Indians who fought against Custer and who rose up again under Dull Knife.

Johnny studied at the Reservation School and he must have gone cold and hungry many times. He refused to give up. He went to high school, too, and I understand that it wasn't easy. There are still a lot of people who are scared of Indians, who take it out by acting nasty, by prejudice. Even poor Indians. Maybe especially poor Indians. But Johnny is no quitter.

He made his grades, high marks always. He entered the Air Force because he wanted to fly, and he made it. In spite of our tradition, there were some cadets who tried to cold shoulder him, to knock him. But that's one thing I'm real proud of. The Air Force doesn't take to that sort of thing. Prejudice plays no part among us . . . and when a man shows it, he'd better hush it up. The brotherhood of the air is a pretty real thing.

Only guy I know who still seems to have some of that cold stuff toward Johnny is Rod Harger. I've heard him make cracks about Redskins when he thought I wasn't listening. I can tell by the way he acts around Johnny what he thinks.

Rod Harger . . . that's a subject I want to give some special thought to. But not now. I might get mad and that'd make my blood pressure climb up.

A shame about Marty, but he'll still have a good career as a pilot. Probably will see him again one of these days.

Those Air Force Intelligence men won't give up. They may take time, but they'll trace that Cessna. When they do, they'll follow through, and someday we're going to find out what that shooting was all about.

The thing is, if somebody is out to whittle down or destroy this team, they're not going to stop there. Most of us are still going. There will be more trouble and right here at Dayton. I'd better talk it over with the fellows, warn everyone to be careful.

But how, of what? How will he strike again?

It's still dark in here and I can't hear a thing. Wonder how many minutes have gone past.

I guess it would be like this in space. Maybe someday I'm going to be in just this same kind of spot. Maybe I'll be in a spaceship, or a space capsule, and the power will fail. I'll be in darkness and there'll be no sound. All around me, just outside the thin metal walls of the ship, there'll be the void of space. No air, just the near vacuum of the emptiness between the planets. There'll be rays in it, vibrations, deadly ones. Lonely particles of elements—molecules, I mean—invisible, indetectable, moving on their incredible orbits across the universe. Meteors, too . . .

And there I'll be. What will I do then? A man could go

crazy under such circumstances. Thousands, maybe millons, of miles from help, surrounded by a little shell of air and metal and nothing else. A dead drop in all directions.

That would be grounds enough for going mad. And that's it exactly. I mustn't. Keep a cool head, and feel around and find out what's wrong. Fix that engine, repair that power system, restore the light. You can't lose your head and do that.

That's why I'm here. The rest of the fellows are going to go through this same thing. They won't all be calm. Some of us are going to get a little jumpy. It would be easy. But not me. I refuse to quit. The road to Mars leads through this dark and silent room. So . . . His thoughts roamed on . . .

There was a flash of light. Mike blinked. The glare hurt his eyes—it was so sudden. There was sound—somewhere voices, somewhere a clanking noise, somewhere a pump going.

"O.K., Samson," said a voice. As his eyes adjusted themselves, Mike saw it was Dr. Holderlin. "Time's up. Come on out. You want to sit there forever?"

Mike got up and waited while one of the doctor's assistants came in and detached the instruments which had recorded his reactions. When Mike stepped out, blinking in the light of the big laboratory room outside the isolation chamber, Dr. Holderlin looked at his charts and nodded.

"You're a very unexciting patient. No interesting leaps and bounds on your tape. Saw no ghosts, eh? And no monsters creeping up behind you either?" He shook his head in mock wonder. "Nerves of iron, young man." He poked Mike with a finger. "But you wait. We got something else maybe we scare you with."

CHAPTER 12

HOODOO PILOT

IT WAS the pattern of the tests to alternate the mental with the physical—thereby keeping a balance and returning the would-be astronauts every night after workouts in both spheres. Yet the fellows managed to enjoy themselves between the tests. The field was a big one, and it was near an interesting city—the birthplace of the Wright Brothers and the original airplane—and the men had time off enough to get in some movies and sight-seeing.

Of course, that was up to them, and Mike and many of the others preferred to hang around the base, to keep themselves in shape, because everything that was happening to them at W.A.D.C. was tricky and required alertness.

But the tests were challenging, too. Mike's comment after a couple of them was, "They ought to be put in amusement parks. I'd bet they'd be a great success."

Lannigan, who had also undergone the two tests in question, laughed. "Yes, but for whom? Not the ones doing it. But it would be fun to watch."

Both young men smiled. It had been fun—after it was all over.

The two tests had both involved the ability to keep a clear head in unexpected situations. One involved quick, correct thinking; the other quick body shifts, a regular balancing act. They complemented each other.

The quick thinking had been a trick control board. Mike was seated at this thing that resembled the control panel of a fast jet. He strapped himself in, the canopy was closed, and he operated the dummy controls which lit the various dials and indicated a proper take-off just as if he were flying. His problem: to keep flying.

What those panels indicated in the next twenty minutes would have turned a veteran pilot's hair gray if they had occurred in real flight. For a while the imaginary plane would be going along all right, and then, bang, a sudden spin. Quick action on the controls to level the plane again, only to find another disaster confronting the pilot—a tailspin, or an inexplicable drop, or a sudden side blast. Mike, during his run, watched the dials like a hawk, trying to outguess the next trick of the imaginary ship. His hands would dart over the controls, pull the stick, swing the ship, take her down, take her up, stall, blast, each to dodge the looming catastrophe registered on his dials.

He never knew so many disasters could occur so fast to any one ship. Yet he realized afterward that each imaginary hoodoo represented something that might come up in rocket flight some day. Speed of reaction, sensible judgment at snap seconds—those were the things being tested here, and the testing may have been dummy but the intent was deadly real.

An astronaut had to be the best and the quickest, or he might never survive. There was too much at stake, and the problems that would be faced in outer space would be emergencies never before anticipated.

Still, once it was over, Mike could appreciate that there was a funny side seen by the observer of the test. Imagine the laughs you could get putting someone through such imaginary disasters.

The other test, the physical one, had its points of similarity. There was a chair mounted on gymbals, which could revolve in all directions. Mike was strapped into it and had nothing to control it but a simple stick, such as was used on the airplanes of forty years ago. Then the thing was started.

No sooner were the holding stabilizers removed than the chair began to slip. Mike had to hold it on an even keel by moving his guide stick in the right direction to bring the chair back straight and level again. Moving the stick even the least bit too far sent the chair off to the other side. Going forward and back, sideways, almost turning over, Mike found himself swiftly balancing the stick, keeping the wildly careening chair upright by the exercise of all his dexterity.

When he thought he had mastered the trick, there began some variations just to throw him off again. There were unexpected new vibrations, new disturbances to the equilibrium, and he had to fight all over again to hold the chair straight and to learn to overcome the annoying new irritations.

When he thought he had had enough of that, the testers blindfolded him and started all over again. By then he had gotten "the feel" of the thing and, though he had a couple of frightening dips at first, he rapidly found his hand reacting correctly.

When he climbed down, he was a little dizzy for a moment

The testers blindfolded him.

but recovered fast. He stuck around the laboratory while Rod Harger followed him. He watched the grim-faced young pilot go through the same gyrations, and it looked funny as all get out—seen from the floor. But from the tight frown on Rod's face Mike knew the pilot wasn't enjoying it.

You had to hand it to Rod, he thought. He was quick at the task. He was a first-class candidate.

But when Rod's test was over and that pale-haired youth stepped down, he gave Mike a look of concentrated anger which made Mike realize that Rod had been aware that he'd been the target of laughter on the part of the other candidates who'd been around.

The piloting test was not the only mental test that day. There were written tests, too, at which the would-be astronauts sat at desks in a regular classroom and answered various sets of trick questions.

The questions were not the kind that would determine how much a student had learned in a term. Some, it is true, did require knowledge, but this was no more than the education they all would have received in high school and in their pre-flight training. Actually, these were intelligence tests not too different from the sort given in any school around the country.

For instance, there was one series known as the Miller Analogies Test. Mike thought it was a snap and a neat little exercise no more difficult than a good game. In a way it was a game. An analogy is a point of resemblance between two things. The test gave two things, which had a type of relationship between them, and then gave a question of choice for something else with the same type of relation. It went like this: *Light* is to *Dark* as *Pleasure* is to *Pain.* But for the word *Pain,* the test gave four choices, each of which had some likely possibility, but only one of which could be completely right.

The first Mike answered on a long list was this: *Joy* is to *Sorrow* as *Laugh* is to (a. *joke,* b. *cry,* c. *grin,* d. *humor*). Unhesitatingly, Mike checked "b." And he was right.

After Mike and the rest had turned in their papers and were dismissed, he and Johnny wandered out to the main landing field to idle around an hour or so before supper and watch the planes. They struck up conversations with several of the officers stationed permanently at the base, and sat around awhile on the porch just outside Base Operations watching the men on duty go in and out, listening to them talk.

Mike was talking to Johnny idly about several of the newer jets which were taxiing down the field to their hangars when he caught a word in a passing pilot's remarks. The word was Cessna. Instantly he turned his head, listened.

Johnny opened his eyes wider and looked, too. Mike got up, caught the arm of the pilot, who was still in his flying suit, and just about to enter the door of Base Ops.

"Excuse me, sir," Mike said, "but did I overhear you say something about a Cessna?"

The pilot stopped, turned. "Sure did, you heard me right. I was talking about that blasted Cessna that was hanging around here this afternoon."

"What was that, sir?" Mike asked. "I didn't hear about it."

The pilot shrugged. "Well, I guess it wasn't much, but it sure screwed me up for a moment. Some fool in a blue Cessna was buzzing the field. I guess he thought it was a private airfield or something. The tower nearly had hysterics ordering the guy away. I was coming down myself then and had to haul up or I'd have hit him for sure."

Mike nodded. "Thanks. Ever see that private plane before, sir?"

The pilot shook his head, "Nah. He's new around here. I've spotted most of the private planes in this neighborhood, but not that one." He went on in.

Mike sat down, looked at Johnny. "Do you suppose that's the man from Colorado?"

Johnny's dark eyes glinted. "I think I'm going to ask the fellows to keep an eye open. I think we better circulate around and ask anybody who spots that plane's field to let us know where it is. It might be interesting to pay its owner a visit."

"My idea exactly," Mike said softly.

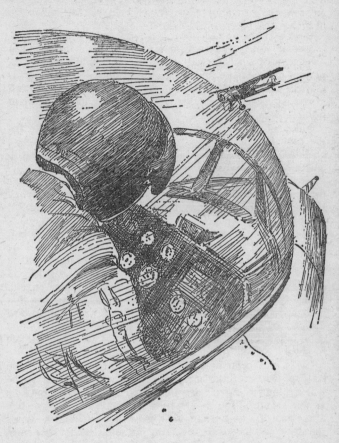

Some fool in a Cessna was buzzing the field.

CHAPTER 13

THE G-FORCE RIDER

"IN SOME ways, gentlemen, this next test is one of the most dangerous of all those you will take. Yet it is also a very important one. Because this machine will tell us—and yourselves as well—just how well you will stand up to the terrible pressures that rocket drive and space flight acceleration are sure to bring."

Mike and the half dozen others who had been selected for the centrifuge tests stood grouped by the wall of the huge chamber while Dr. Holderlin briefed them. Mike looked with curiosity and interest at this remarkable device.

At first sight he could think only of a big carnival wheel—the kind that swings you around in little cabs—like a sort of Ferris wheel laid on its side. Undoubtedly the inventors of this thing had been inspired by such circus engines.

A circular rail ran around the roof of the huge chamber. A powerful engine in the center of the room drove a long metal arm, perhaps fifty feet in length, around the room on this arm like the hand of a giant clock. Hanging near the end of this crane was a small metal and glass cabin large enough to seat one man. It was so attached to the revolving arm that it could be made to swing in closer to the center or out toward the end of the crane, thereby enabling the operator of the contraption to slow it down or speed it up according to how far away he chose to put it from the rotating center.

"This is a centrifuge, and the man to be tested will be strapped into the little enclosed seat. When the arm starts he will find himself moving around the room at the end of the long arm. Now all of you have seen a boy swing a rock or a stick at the end of a long string. You know that the faster he twirls the string and the longer the string is, the faster that rock must move. So it is with this device, only you will be the rock. Fortunately it is wide enough so that dizziness will not itself be a problem. Something else will be."

The doctor paused, looked at them. The young fellows stared around at the centrifuge intently and listened with care.

"You already know something about what is called G-force.

Mike could think only of a big carnival wheel.

You have experienced it in your flying, but I am going to explain it again. Your weight is determined by the pull of gravity. And when we figure your weight on the surface of the Earth we say it is one G.

"Now when you accelerate, when you start moving faster and faster, you move against gravity and you add to your own weight. So, when you are gathering speed fast enough, by and by you find that your weight has doubled, you now have to endure two G's. Speed up even more—and I don't mean just travel at a fast speed, but increase your speed faster—and you will get three G's. Keep it up and your weight increases all the time—four, five, six G's, and so on.

"In the Air Force you wear these special G-suits when you

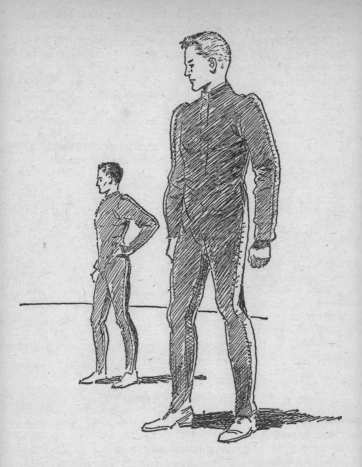

fly such rapidly accelerating planes as jet planes because the planes accelerate so fast that you gather G's quickly. Naturally this is not so good for your body. Your bones and flesh are used to carrying around only their own natural weight. If we make it easy and say that you weigh a hundred pounds, at two G's already you weigh two hundred pounds. This is hard on the body, but it can stand it because the increased weight is evenly divided all over, and your body is strongly made, believe me. But you can see that if you are carrying six G's, then you weigh six hundred pounds and this is no joke. Lift your hand alone and you lift a heavy weight with it.

"Now the problem with rockets is that they accelerate very fast. They just don't work more gently. So whoever is going to fly a rocket to the moon, he is going to have to endure a terrible strain during the first few minutes of that ride. Maybe eight or even nine G's. This could be very deadly, you can imagine.

"Of course, you will have protection, as much as possible, but even so . . ."

Mike pursed his lips, looked at the little cabin hanging so innocently at the end of its crane. Dr. Holderlin went on:

"Fortunately for science we have a way of testing you out for your reaction to G-forces that is a lot safer then sending you off in a rocket at once. This centrifuge swings you around fast enough so that you get the same effect exactly by means of centrifugal force. We can watch you as the G's rise, see how you are, how much you can take. And you yourself will know what it is like, what you will go through. Strange things happen sometimes. It is even dangerous. So . . . who is willing to go first?" He glanced at the silent young men.

Mike thought to himself, if I wait and watch someone else, I might get scared; let's get this over with. He stepped forward, said quietly, "I'm game."

The doctor nodded. "Ah, it's our impetuous young man from Mars again, so? He arrives late and wants to leave early, eh?"

There were chuckles from the other fellows. Mike grinned a little nervously. "Well, come on," said the doctor, and led him over to the little cabin.

There were a couple of engineers directing the thing from a plastic bubble in the ceiling. The cabin dipped down, and the doctor opened it. Mike, who, like the other fellows, was wearing his flying G-suit, padded against dangerous acceleration, squeezed in, and the doctor and an assistant strapped him in.

The transparent window right in front of him gave him a limited view, and he saw that there was the eye of a camera mounted before him. Pictures would be taken, and by split-second lighting the observers could watch his progress.

When he felt secure, he heard the doctor's voice in his earphones. "All set?" Mike nodded.

The crane began to move and the cabin started to follow it around the great chamber. It turned, faced the direction of its drive. For a time it didn't feel bad, rather like riding in a comfortable car. After circling the room a few times at a reasonable pace, Mike felt it begin to move faster. Not only were the walls flashing past him more and more but he also felt himself being drawn back in his seat, pressing against the cushions.

So far so good, though. Like a car making a fast getaway, he thought. Doesn't hurt. Maybe getting to two G's.

Steadily the great crane gathered momentum, and the cabin whistling around the room gained speed. Mike felt himself being pressed hard against the seat, his arms against the padded arms. He saw that the straps of his suit were tight and he felt the compensating pressure of the remarkable G-suit beginning to assert itself.

Steadily the pressure grew, and what at first had seemed almost comfortable became unpleasant. He found that it was becoming hard to breathe. He had to consciously force his lungs up and down, and he realized that the weight of his ribs was burdensome—perhaps now he had three times his own weight to carry and it was hard.

In his ears he felt his heart begin to pound harder. Still the pressure grew. The walls outside were spinning past now as if he were in a hurtling, racing car. It became a struggle to keep on breathing, a matter of deliberate hard work, of conscious effort. He tried raising his hand, found it heavy—heavy as if many pounds of lead were resting on it, on every finger.

Now he fought to keep control of his face. He felt his lips trembling as the pressure on his body grew. Finally he felt them draw away, but he pressed them back against his teeth. He wanted to let his mouth drop open. Something was pressing against his eyeballs.

The acceleration grew. Dimly, through the roaring in his ears, he heard the doctor's voice say, "This is four G's. You are doing very well. We are watching; don't be afraid. We continue."

He wondered how much more he could take. But he felt he was mastering the art of breathing. His eyes hurt, but he held them open, and his lips were still sealed.

He felt the acceleration increase again. He concentrated, held on. How high would it go? More and more his heart was pounding and his lungs felt tired and the muscles of his chest hurt. He couldn't hold his lips back, they pulled away from his teeth, flaring back as if held by a dentist's instruments. He could not close them. His teeth were tight together.

His eyes were paining now; he felt as if something were pressing hard steel fingers into his eyeballs. The flesh of his cheeks and face was being pushed back, probed back by the same invisible steely fingers.

He looked through eyes that could no longer blink and he saw the straight lines of the frame of the metal-rimmed window suddenly bend down, swing at a slant. How could that be? he thought dazedly to himself. But they were moving, slanting and twisting even more.

Now at last things began to go gray. He saw the window with its strangely warped frame begin to dim out, to be lost in a quickly gathering fog. Then he blacked out.

He came to in a few seconds to find the pressure already greatly eased up. He looked around, closed his lips, and felt his flesh resuming its normal flexibility—the steely fingers had gone. And the window—it was straight again; somehow the twisted rims had snapped back. I must ask the doctor how that was done, he thought.

Then it was over. The centrifuge was at rest. An assistant ran over and opened the door of the cabin. As the doctor came up, Mike was already unstrapped and, with the assistant's hand on his arm to steady him, he stepped down to the floor.

Dr. Holderlin quickly looked at his face. Mike felt momentarily dizzy, but more than that he felt weak, drained as if he had been through an ordeal—as he had.

"Very good," the doctor was saying. "Very good. And no injuries. Not even red spots in the eyes from broken blood vessels. I think you do fine."

Mike walked a little unsteadily over to a bench by the wall. "That wasn't so bad," he said, "now that it's over. But, doctor, how did you work that window twisting trick?"

He sat down. The doctor looked down at him, puzzled. "Explain, please. What did you see?"

Mike explained. For a moment the doctor was still baffled, scratched his head, then suddenly he laughed. "Ah, I see. You make a mistake. The window frame never changed itself, it was solid all the time and it never bent at all. There was no window trick."

"But I saw it, plain and clear with my own eyes," said Mike. "I didn't imagine it."

Dr. Holderlin grew serious. "You did, and what you saw was exactly what your eyes saw. That is one of the dangers of space flight. Because it was not the window and the frame that bent down, twisted itself. It was your *eye* that was twisted.

The pressure at that point bent the very lenses of your eyes—and a bent lens gets a bent picture! Someday out in space under acceleration you might see things that are not there—and you should never forget this lesson here."

Mike told himself he never would. For he had seen that frame bend itself as clearly and surely as you can see this page before your eyes—and it was still an illusion.

CHAPTER 14

THE HOT SIDE OF MERCURY

YET that centrifuge test was not quite the strangest Mike had to go through. There were a number of clever tests all designed to determine the limits of his ability to stand up under heavy and unusual strain. Many of the other candidates were beginning to look a little peaked from what they were doing. In the evenings a lot of fellows would just go right to bed after suppertime to rest up from whatever they had gone through or in anticipation of what was to come.

Not all the tests were given in the same order—usually these various devices, such as the dark chamber and the centrifuge, could only take one man at a time. So some men had not yet gone through these tests and others had already undergone some that Mike would be facing. There was no great secret about it, and the fellows would often compare experiences.

"You been swung around today?" Jack Lannigan asked Mike that night at the supper table. When Mike nodded, Jack shook his head. "I had it yesterday and, boy, what a time! But I'd do it again rather than face the hot box I had this morning. I bet I lost five pounds then. Drank like crazy when it was over."

"Hot box?" said Mike. "What's that?" Johnny Bluehawk and several others within hearing leaned over.

"Oh," said Jack, seizing the opportunity to throw a slight scare into the others, "it's just that you get baked in an oven for a couple hours."

"You get what!" Mike said. "Baked?"

"It's a heat test," the young Navy pilot explained. "They sit you down in a little room, close the door, and run the heat up to 130 degrees Fahrenheit. Then they keep it there for two hours, just to see how you stand it. Of course, they have the usual check on your heart and breathing, but, believe me, you can perspire like you never did."

Mike took a forkful of pie. "I guess they think we might get a little hot in outer space, like say traveling near the sun, or having the cooling system get a little haywire. How did you stand it?"

Jack shook his head. "I didn't like it, but I guess the system can stand it—a little while at least. You have to consider there are places in the tropics or the desert where that kind of temperature is fairly regular in the summer, yet people and animals survive. It gets very uncomfortable. At first it seems easy, just cozy and hot. But by and by you start to get wet with perspiration, and soon you're all damp and still feel hot. After a little longer you get kind of dry and baked out, and I felt a little bit dizzy by the time the wait was over.

"I just sat there and daydreamed. It would be awful, though, to have to go through that in a small spaceship cabin for days at a time."

"If we had to, I guess we'd just manage," Mike remarked. He looked around at all the fellows at the various tables in the mess hall. "Where's Carroll and McNair?" he asked. "Don't see them here."

Jack looked up from his plate, gave him a sharp glance. "Haven't you heard? They're in the infirmary, pretty badly banged up."

Johnny Bluehawk frowned. "I did hear something, but I was waiting my turn at the centrifuge. I guess Mike was going up in it then. What was the story?"

Jack Lannigan put down his fork. "You know, come to think of it, it was mighty strange. Carroll and McNair were to take up a plane for the weightlessness run today. They were walking out to their plane, out on the field, when an F-89 Scorpion came taxiing in from the landing run. The darn fool piloting it came rushing up on them, all wild and wobbly. The thing spun around, trying to stop, and almost hit the two head on. They tried to run, but it turned wildly and they got slapped by a wing tank. A little closer and they could have gotten blasted by the exhaust as well."

Mike stopped eating. "That's the craziest thing I ever heard of. What kind of a pilot could do something like that? It doesn't sound possible unless it was deliberate."

"That's it," said Jack. "The two fellows are laid up pretty badly. Nothing they won't get over with—a couple broken ribs, a cracked elbow—but it puts them out of the show here. They don't know who the pilot was either."

"I heard something about that," said Johnny. "The fellow just got out of the plane, in his oxygen mask and helmet and goggles, and walked off, while the rest of the men around were rushing the two fellows to the infirmary. Now they can't find who he was. The man assigned to that F-89 swears he was never out on the field at all, and wasn't due to take the ship up for another half hour."

Mike looked at Johnny. "The driver of that wild car in San Antonio, the sniper in Colorado, the man in the blue Cessna seen here a couple days ago. Someone's out to get the best men."

The three exchanged glances. "Better watch our steps," Mike said after a moment. "He won't have too much longer to do his dirty work."

The next day was Mike's turn at the hot box and it was every bit as uncomfortable as Jack Lannigan had said. Mike managed to keep himself from thinking about his discomfort by just sitting in the chair as motionless as possible and imagining himself assigned to an astronomical station on the sunny side of Mercury.

Mercury, so close to the sun, with one side always turned toward that blazing great globe in its airless sky, would be a red-hot assignment someday for America's astronauts. It would be invaluable as a place to study the sun from, and the conditions of terrible heat that prevailed on its sunward side would surely hold many remarkable chemical and physical secrets for men to discover. But it would be like this . . . just heat and more heat, and men would have to endure it.

So he endured it, and after it was over he made a fast enough recovery.

He was looking forward to the weightlessness test, but that would not come for him and Johnny for another couple of days. So he faced more of the endurance problems.

There were some funny ones. There was the tilt table, for instance. They had a table you had to lie down on. Then they tilted it until you were hanging at a steep slant, and they left you there for a half hour just to see how your heart would act to make up for the strange slant of your body.

Then there was the business of the ice water. "Take your shoes and stockings off, and shove your feet quickly into the tub of ice water." It was a shock, of course, and Dr. Holderlin's assistants doubtless made some important measurements of your pulse and blood pressure while you were doing it. It wasn't fun, but it didn't hurt and was over soon.

There was another pressure chamber test the following day. In this one Mike had to put on a partial pressure suit, the MC1 model, and be taken to the altitude equivalent of 65,000 feet. He had had things like this before, and the experience at

Mount Evans stood him in good stead. He took the hour without any trouble at all.

That day, which was to be the final one before his own no-gravity flight, ended with more written tests. Mike was glad to see the day end, for he was looking forward to the next day's experience. He had been grounded for too long during these tests, and he was hungry to feel a plane under him, to get up into the wide clean air, to rush on like a bullet into the sky and leave the earth below. Too, he had read so many stories in his young life about space flight that he wanted to see what the experience of not feeling any gravity would be like at long last.

He was hungry to feel a plane under him.

The written tests this time were really odd. Brain-teasers in a different sense, Mike thought, because they were tests that had no correct answers and were judged solely by what you were thinking when you answered them.

For instance, there was this one: a whole series of unfinished sentences was given. Mike had to finish each one, and it was hard to figure out what to say. They ran like this: "I am sorry that . . ." "I can never . . ." "I hope . . ."

There was no clue as to what you were supposed to say, because you were supposed to say anything at all that seemed to fit. Mike sucked his pencil when he got them, then took the plunge and went on to write whatever seemed to make a sensible, truthful answer.

He never did know what the doctors thought of his answers, but since they didn't come after him with the net, he figured he was thinking straight. Since Mike had trained himself from boyhood never to deceive himself, always to think honestly and to look squarely at the facts, whatever they were, this wasn't at all surprising.

CHAPTER 15

UPHILL CLIMB

THE morning of that last big day began with what could have been a long hike, except that Mike never left the room in which he was walking. But he certainly felt that he had gone miles, because this was the treadmill test and it was just about as exhausting as climbing a steep mountain.

Mike, trimmed down to shorts and light shoes, was walking on a short moving belt on a platform in one of the examination laboratories. Attachments to his arms registered his heartbeat and blood pressure as he walked; and he was walking at a steady, strong, fast rate, a good normal hiking speed indeed.

One of Dr. Holderlin's assistants was watching him, registering the changes in his physical capacity, and every minute adjusting the moving platform so that it was one degree higher. The effect was that when Mike started walking it was as if he were on level ground. But each minute and each elevation made the ground slope gradually upward, so that after a half hour he was walking uphill and getting a steadily steeper climb.

Mike could walk on a level all day, if he had to. He'd always been a good hiker, because long ago he had found it was a wonderful way of getting exercise naturally, of keeping in trim, and of allowing himself to let his thoughts wander onto the space lanes he hoped to travel someday.

He tramped on and on and the studious young attendant kept making the walk harder and harder. Mike felt himself getting tired in spite of his efforts, for the higher the platform tilted the more energy he had to use to take each step. A thin sweat was developing on his body, but he trudged on, and as usual his mind was taking him away from his growing discomfort into realms of thought.

There was some purpose behind the strange attacks on the men of Project Quicksilver, he was thinking. As far as he could figure out, it would be the desire to eliminate unfairly as many good contestants as possible. Now the only ground for this would be that some one of the men, who might not otherwise be among the top seven, would have a better chance. He couldn't help but think that the only fellow likely to try such a dirty trick would be Rod Harger.

His heart pounding harder, Mike kept on trudging, while the attendant stood back watching him quizzically. But Mike was no quitter and, though the platform was really now quite steep, he kept on mechanically, turning over in his mind the possible chances for further deviltry against himself and his friends.

Now, while Mike was going through this tiresome test, the man he was thinking about, Rod Harger, was in a private phone booth elsewhere on the base. He was talking to his father. He listened silently for a while, nodding or saying yes. Then he said, "Your man takes his time, and he hasn't much left. There are still two or three fellows I'm uneasy about. You know who. I gave him their names."

He listened more. "Yes, well, tell your man he'd better move today. Two of them, Mars and that Indian, are going up this afternoon in a no-gravity flight. That'll be the last of their tests; the rest of the candidates have been up or are going up today, also."

He listened, then smiled hard. "O.K., I'm counting on you. Get your man into action . . . Yes, I know he took a chance on the field, but he may have to again. O.K., dad." He hung up, looked around to see if anyone he knew had observed his call, and, seeing no one, stepped out of the booth and walked quietly away. He himself had already had his testing, and he was confident he'd done all right. There was nothing wrong physically with Rod, but he'd learned the wrong lesson. He didn't believe in playing fair.

Back in the lab building, Mike began to feel himself getting a little worn. Just then, the attendant who had been watching the heartbeat register carefully, reached out and dropped the platform to level. "O.K., test's over," he announced. "Your heartbeat's up to 180 a minute and that's enough for us."

Mike stepped down, grabbed a towel, and wiped the sweat off his chest and brow. "Whew," he said, "I'm glad that's over." He sat down for a few minutes to rest, then got up and went to the cafeteria in a nearby building to have some lunch. When he walked in, he found several of the fellows already there, including Johnny Bluehawk. He got himself a sandwich and a glass of milk and went over and joined them.

"Walk a mile and rest awhile," Johnny sang softly as he sat down. "A million and one miles to go."

"Yep," said Mike, "that was it. I see you had yours this morning, too."

The Cheyenne nodded and other fellows in hearing smiled in reminiscence. "Some of the boys think that was the hardest of them all. Personally it didn't seem that way to me. I hated the heat room most."

Mike took a bite and, while he was chewing, thought the tests over. "I dunno," he said after a while. "They all seemed hard, but it was always possible to go through it. I think I didn't really like some of the just plain medical probing they did back in Texas."

There was a general guffaw of laughter. "I guess most of the guys agree with you," Johnny grinned.

Then he suddenly sobered. "I almost forgot. I think we have a line on the whereabouts of that blue Cessna plane. One of the airmen we'd asked to look for it says he was driving on a back road somewhere in the Germantown area and passed what looked like an old farm. He says he thinks he saw a blue plane parked out on an open meadow near a big barn there. Couldn't see it plain, but it looked like a Cessna."

Mike leaned forward. "Did you get the exact location?"

The Cheyenne took a slip of paper from his pocket. "I got the directions for it. If we have a few hours to ourselves tomorrow, let's borrow a car and look for it."

Mike nodded, "Yes, only maybe we can talk Colonel Drummond into letting us borrow a plane instead. It'd be much easier to spot from the air."

Johnny agreed. "It's a deal. Meanwhile, we got some very special flying today. I'm to pilot you on the first set of tests, you know. Shall we go over and get into our flight suits?"

Mike finished his milk, wiped his lips. "I'm set," he said, and the two got up and strolled out.

Seated at a nearby table was a tall, thin man wearing the uniform of a flight lieutenant. He had apparently been drinking a cup of coffee, but if anyone had cared to took they would have found that he had not taken a sip during this conversation. Instead he had been listening very intently to what the two would-be astronauts were saying. Now that they had left, he put the cup down, carefully got up, keeping his back to the others at the candidates' table, and went quietly out. There was a sly smile on his bony face, and the curious hooked scar on his right cheek was drawn taut, as if the man were under some kind of tension.

At the Base Operations building, the two friends checked in at the desk, got their assignment call, and went down to the equipment room. They were issued their jet-flight suits and, after going into the locker room, changed into their flying clothes, pulling on the warm coveralls and the padded G-suits, picked up their leather helmets and fitted them on, and then took their big covering white protective helmets under their arms.

Mike had, as usual, carefully painted his initials, M.A.R.S., on the front of his helmet. As for Johnny, he had removed a little envelope from his locker, taken out a small blue feather, and taped it to the side of his.

From the early days of flying, back during the wild days of the Lafayette Squadron and the Spads of World War I, right up to the present, pilots have had their little special luck pieces and superstitions. Mike wasn't superstitious, but he didn't see any harm in going along with the tradition. Besides, he liked to remind himself of his final goal every time he went up for a flight.

As for Johnny, well, it was a delicate subject to figure out just how many strange things he might have been brought up to believe. But he never flew without that feather or one like it. When he was a fledgling student pilot he wasn't allowed to wear it on his uniform, but he carried it in his pocket. Now he wore it openly on his helmet.

They stomped out of the locker room and back to the operations desk in their clumsy outfits, lugging their parachutes under their arms and their oxygen masks as well. They sat down to await the arrival of Colonel Drummond. As they were sitting, a man in a lieutenant's uniform came over carrying a small tray and two cups of coffee. He looked at them, then set the tray down.

"You must be the boys going to take the anti-gravity flight. The other fellows in the cafeteria sent over the coffee. They say you'll need it. Better drink up."

Mike and Johnny looked at him in surprise, then laughed. "Those characters and their gags," said Johnny, "but I do feel like a cup before going up." He picked up one of the steaming cups, stirred it a bit, and slowly drank it. "Hmm, hits the spot," he said. He turned to the man who had brought the coffee, but he had left. He looked around at Mike, as he was finishing the hot drink. "Aren't you going to have yours?" he asked his friend.

Mike shook his head. "I just never got into the coffee habit, and I don't think I will even for this operation. It was darned nice of that fellow to take these over to us, though. Wonder who he was?"

The Cheyenne looked blank. "I never saw him before either. Well, maybe we'll run into him again someday, and then we can thank him."

He put his empty cup down. He didn't know it, and neither did Mike, but they had both run into that "lieutenant" before —and they would someday see him again, but not the way they imagined.

CHAPTER 16

BEYOND THE GRIP OF GRAVITY

OUT on the field the two young pilots found Colonel Drummond waiting for them beside the jet they were to use. It was a twin-jet T-37, a kind with which the two were familiar, for it had been one they had used in their early training period.

"I assume you were at the general briefing held two days ago on this weightlessness maneuver," the colonel said. "I trust you remember the fundamentals of this test."

"Yes, sir," said Mike. "We were there. It sounds like an interesting experience."

"Interesting? Well, that will depend on how it affects you," the colonel nodded. "Which of you will pilot first?"

"I will, sir," said Johnny Bluehawk. "When we come down, we will then reverse seats and Mike Mars—I mean Lieutenant Samson—will pilot me."

The colonel shot a glance at Mike, then looked again at the young Cheyenne. "And what will you do? Do you remember how you are supposed to handle this test?"

The Indian glanced at the big silver jet, which was obviously all fueled, checked, and ready to go, judging from the watchful stares of the ground crew. "I do, sir," he replied.

"I shall take her up to about 20,000 feet, start down, then bring her up sharply and swing into a parabolic curve. Done correctly, this should have the effect of countering gravity with an equally strong centrifugal force . . . and if the swing is wide enough and fast enough this effect should last somewhere between twenty and forty seconds. I'm sure I can do it the first time, sir. I've heard it described often."

The colonel nodded, turned to Mike. "Now I want you to remember everything you feel during these tests, and right afterward describe your feelings to your pilot. On your return to the ground you will be expected to write them down in a complete report. I want you to make a series of such tests. On the first swing, keep your eyes open; on the second, keep your eyes closed; on the third, let something drop from your hands and let your arms swing loose; on the fourth swing, look outside the ship."

"I understand, sir," said Mike, reaching into a flap of his flying suit and producing a pencil. "I'll use this for a drop."

"O.K., then," said the colonel. "Take her on up."

The two climbed into the plane. The T-37 seated two men side by side, differing in this respect from most jet-fighters. In this specially prepared ship, the pilot sat in the right seat, the passenger to undergo the test in the left seat. There had once been dual controls opposite the left seat; but now it faced an empty dashboard, because the stick and instruments had been removed. Consequently, there was a little more space for arm and leg motion than would usually be available in a jet cockpit.

Johnny strapped himself in, checked his meters and his earphones. Mike climbed in, strapped himself in lightly, and felt slightly useless as he realized that he was to be just a passenger, and a pretty helpless one at that.

Johnny put the ship into motion, taxied gently to the runway designated by the tower. The transparent canopy was slid shut and fastened. Once up in the air, the only way they could escape in the event of emergency would be to pull the little yellow lever which would cause the explosive ejection of the entire seat unit. Only after that could they safely parachute down. Mike noted out of the corner of his eye that in this altered ship the ejection lever was available only on the pilot's side.

The T-37 waited at the runway for take-off orders. Mike looked around, looked at his companion. Johnny seemed preoccupied with meters, then his head snapped up. "Everything O.K.?" Mike asked, talking over his radiophone connection.

"Mmmm," Johnny said. "Oh, ah, yes. Sure."

Mike looked at him. "You sleepy?" he asked sharply. The Indian jerked his head up. "No, no. Just for a moment I was sort of daydreaming. Nerves, I guess."

Mike looked over at him silently. Nerves, indeed. He'd never known Johnny to show signs of nervousness before. But, he supposed, even if the Cheyenne was a bit distracted, when he started breathing oxygen, it'd clear his head.

The tower gave the order. Both boys were pushed back into their seats as the fast training jet, under its twin engine drive, roared upward into the sky.

Mike adjusted his oxygen mask, Johnny did the same. Upward they climbed, and Mike, leaning over, could see the altimeter registering the distance from the earth in rapidly climbing figures.

Now at a little over 20,000 feet they leveled off. "Ready?" said Johnny. "I'm going to dive to gather speed. Then, at 17,-

000 feet, I'm bringing her nose up sharply and climbing into a wide humped curve. That'll be it."

"O.K., I'm with you," said Mike, bracing himself into his seat.

The ship's nose dipped down suddenly and with screaming jets the big silver plane roared down toward the ground below at a sixty-five-degree angle. Faster and faster it went, and Mike felt himself pressed hard in his seat, just as he had been in the centrifuge test. From the pressure of his skin and the weight of his hands, he estimated that he had about three G's on him.

Now, like a madman, Johnny pulled the nose of the ship back, started climbing upwards at a sixty-degree climb at full throttle, and began a wide pushover.

Mike, at first crushed into his seat by the force of the dive, suddenly found the pressure gone. He felt himself swinging loose in his seat as the climb overcame the force of gravity's pull, as the centrifugal force of the ship's parabolic curve countered the downward drag of the earth below.

Now he was weightless. His body was simultaneously being thrust upward by the force of the outward swinging ship and being pulled downward by gravity, and with the delicate balance of each, his weight was entirely cancelled.

Johnny deserved credit, he thought in a split second. Most fliers don't quite succeed in getting the touch of it at once. A darned good pilot.

He found himself swinging loosely in his seat. He slipped the straps that held him to give himself more space, and he floated an inch above the padded seat. He moved his hands before him, twisted his head, and thought about his feelings.

Gosh, it was nice, he thought. I feel good, real good. And restful. It's like floating in a dream, it's so relaxing, so pleasant. Nothing pushing him, nothing pulling him, just floating light as a feather—lighter in fact.

So this is what it would be like in a spaceship. Just gently floating about with no pressure on me. So calm, so good. Gee, this is fun.

Mike remembered that he was supposed to take note of how his body felt. It was so pleasant, though. Well, now that he thought of it, there was a sort of tingly feeling in his middle, just a little bit of giddiness around his stomach. Not bad, he thought, not bad at all.

I'm breathing fast, though, he noted to himself. And seem to have a little faint perspiration now.

He glanced at Johnny. The pilot was intent on his dials, hand firm on the control. Mike knew Johnny would also be experiencing weightlessness sensations, but his tight seat strapping and concentration would prevent him from noticing all that Mike had time to notice. Johnny seemed all right, though.

The swing lasted maybe thirty seconds, but it seemed a long time to Mike. It was so pleasant that he almost regretted it when he felt himself pulling back into his seat and saw that the ship was nosing down again, roaring toward the ground.

"Seventeen thousand feet again, Mike," said Johnny's voice. "I'm taking her up and over once more. This is the second round."

"Right," said Mike. "How'd you like it?"

"Didn't notice," said Johnny. "You're supposed to tell me. Now close your eyes on this hump."

Mike felt the pressure on his straps let up again as the plane roared up in another parabolic curve. He shut his eyes tightly.

Again he felt good. With his eyes closed it was even more like dreaming, like a dream in which you float softly across the countryside, never touching the ground. Mike just floated, his body not touching the seat, the straps relaxed.

I'm in outer space, he thought. I'm heading for Mars in a big rocket ship and floating on momentum between the planets. I'm in a celestial orbit, he thought, and one of these days my ship is going to cross Mars' orbit and I'll be there. This is what it will feel like.

He floated on, eyes closed. His stomach, his skin, his breath were acting the same way—just a little bit of tingling all around. Really not at all bad.

He felt elated; he laughed slightly to himself. In his earphones he could hear the deep breathing of Johnny Bluehawk, his pilot, but there was no comment. "Michael Mars is my name . . ." Mike said in a happy singsong tone. He felt like saying aloud his private little poem, the one he'd made up when just a kid in junior high.

He felt himself pressed against his seat. The curve was over; the ship was heading down again. He opened his eyes. The ground was ahead of him, the T-37 was roaring on down.

"America's my nation," said Mike, repeating unintentionally the next line of his poem, "but I don't want to get plastered all over its landscape right now. Time to pull her up for the next curve, Johnny."

He felt himself forced into his seat as the roaring twin jets combined with the pull of gravity to speed the silver ship faster and faster toward the earth. He shot a glance over to the next seat. Johnny was slumped down in his seat, apparently staring at the controls. With his helmet and his mask on, it was hard to see his face.

"Johnny?" Mike said. Then, "Johnny!" he called sharply.

But there was no reply. Just the sound of deep breathing in his earphones and the faint hint of a snore.

Johnny Bluehawk had fallen asleep! And the ship was racing toward the ground at full throttle.

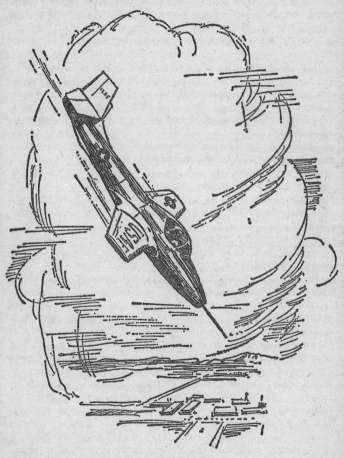

The ship was racing toward the ground!

CHAPTER 17

SPLIT SECONDS

IN AN instant Mike snapped open the catch that held his seat strap down. He felt himself being pressed into the back of his seat by the growing force of the diving plane, but he lurched out of his seat, fighting the pressure and weight of his own body.

The plane was diving straight down, gathering speed as it went. Mike knew that the ship would tear itself apart if it reached too great a speed and that he must act at once to pull it out. But the controls were reached only from the next seat, which was blocked by the bulky suited body of his unconscious buddy.

He cried out, "Johnny!" as loud as he could; but if the sleeping pilot heard him, he was too drugged to answer.

He lurched across the seat, pushed himself across the young Indian's body. This made the seat too crowded for him to grasp the control stick. Hastily he grabbed for the catch of Johnny's suit, snapped the safety belt loose. The force of the diving plane held Johnny in his seat.

Mike dragged at his arm, pulled him over. Slowly, it seemed, though it must have been in but split seconds, the bulky, masked, and helmeted form slid over on its side.

In Mike's earphones he could hear the ground officer calling from below, "Pull out of that dive, fast!"

But Mike didn't answer. He fell across Johnny's body to reach the controls, grab the stick. As he did so, his mind, still coolly alert, ran off another line of his brave little personal poem. "Space flying is my game . . ." He must have said it aloud, for the voice in his earphones from the ground, now frantic, was calling, "Bluehawk, pull out!" And as it did so, another voice, that of Colonel Drummond, cut in, shouting in haste: "Mike Mars—eject! That's an order—eject at once!"

But Mike had no intention of ejecting. To pull the little yellow lever, now so close to his reach by the pilot's seat, would save his life, for it would explode the charge hidden beneath the two seats and throw the seats and the two men in them far out from the plunging plane. Mike could then open his parachute and drift safely to the ground, while the plane buried itself in a roar of exploding, blazing ruin into the ground it must be approaching so fast and so violently. But it would not help his buddy, Johnny Bluehawk. Unconscious, the young Indian would simply fall to the earth with unopened parachute or else be snagged in the seat capsule, for now he was lying along the flooring of the plane, jammed nearly under the seat by the force of the steady acceleration.

Mike clung to the stick, pulled it back.

The roaring, diving plane quivered, fought violently, then gradually its nose pulled up. Mike found himself being crushed back painfully against the seat across which he was lying. He fought to hold his head from striking the arm, which was being pressed against him. He felt his legs rising into the air from the viciously shifting G-forces of the plane's pull-up.

But the plane pulled out, roared up again, rising at a thirty-degree angle at top speed.

Mike fell across the seat, then scrambled himself across Johnny's crumpled body and squeezed himself into the pilot's seat. Reaching out, he cut down the throttle, easing off the screaming twin jets; and while he did this, he said triumphantly to himself, "And Mars my destination!"

He glanced out now for the first time at the earth. It had been close, he realized with a shock. He must have come as close as two hundred feet to the ground before the plane had come out of its dive. All the time that dive had been doing on, Mike had simply banished all thought of the earth—but now he felt a cold sweat come over him as he realized how dreadfully near he had been to total catastrophe.

Colonel Drummond's voice was still on the tower radio, calling angrily, demanding an answer. Mike swung the ship around in a wide circle, preparing to bring it down. "This is Mike Mars," he said, "I mean—Samson, sir. It's under control now. Give me my landing instructions. Lieutenant Bluehawk is unconscious, sir. Drugged, I think."

After he received the O.K. to bring the T-37 down, he answered Drummond's query by recounting the curious incident of the coffee. It was immediately apparent to Mike that Johnny, who had never been sick to his knowledge, had been given something in that coffee.

The plane landed, and as it rolled up, an ambulance was waiting. Medics swiftly swarmed into the plane and lifted Johnny Bluehawk out. Johnny was beginning to stir now, and as they set him down on the stretcher, he opened his eyes and looked around.

The medic in charge bent over him, rolled up his eyelid, looked into his mouth, listened to his heart. Johnny was still sort of sluggish, for he mumbled something and went to sleep again.

Colonel Drummond came charging up to the grounded plane in a yellow field jeep. He arrived in time to hear the medic say to Mike, "No doubt of it, he seems drugged. Otherwise he's all right. He'll come out of it in a little while, but we'll remove him to the infirmary for a checkup and maybe a stomach pump."

The colonel was furious. His weather-lined gray eyes sparked with emotion. "This is another act of sabotage. An outrage! This has got to be stopped!"

He grabbed Mike by the shoulder. "I'm glad you blocked that attempt, but next time don't take the chance. When I say eject, I mean it. We can't afford to waste good men with heroics!"

Mike stiffened. "Sir, I couldn't eject while I had a chance to save Bluehawk. I knew I could get control of the ship, and I would never have forgiven myself if I hadn't tried."

Colonel Drummond stared at him, shook his head in wonder. "I guess you knew what you could do. But, next time, obey orders anyway."

Mike wasn't through, however. Now that he was on the ground, he felt himself getting angry, not at the plane, not at the colonel, but at the scurvy, murderous trick. "Sir," he said, "there may be a chance that that fake lieutenant"—he had not hesitated to assume without thinking that the man must have been a fake, for no Air Force man could have done such a thing—"may still be on the base. No time should be lost looking for him."

The colonel nodded. "I've already given orders to find him. But I don't think he'll be around. He's had time to make his getaway."

Mike bit his lip, "Then, sir, I'd like permission to take a plane right away and go to look for that mysterious blue Cessna. It was connected with the shooting in Colorado and it was seen here. It's our only lead to this killer."

The colonel was clearly as furious as Mike was. He glanced at Mike, saw the angry determination in the young man's face. "Blast it," he said, "yes. If you know where to look for it, find it."

The colonel turned on his heel, swept the field with his eyes.

There were many planes lined up on the field, but not all were ready to fly. He heard a throbbing from one plane far down the line. It was a T-33, a T-Bird getting ready to take off.

Colonel Drummond jumped into the jeep, and Mike jumped in beside him. "Get to that T-Bird before she gets away!" he told the driver and the little yellow car raced madly down the field.

They reached the T-Bird as it was slowly rolling toward the

He had a rendezvous with a killer.

runway. The colonel stood up in the jeep, waved it to a stop. The single-seater jet halted; the pilot threw back the canopy.

There was a quick conversation between the pilot and the colonel, which ended with the pilot climbing out and Mike Mars climbing into his place. The pilot, who had been going on a routine mission, paused as he passed Mike to slap him on the back. "Go to it, fellow and catch that skunk!" Like everyone else on the field, he had overheard the radiophone conversation and witnessed the near disaster.

Mike Mars slid into the seat, buckled himself in, slid the canopy shut. He fumbled inside his clothes and came up with the slip of paper on which the airman had jotted the place he had seen the blue Cessna. Scanning it, he nodded, threw in his throttle, and taxied down to the take-off.

He had a rendezvous with a killer.

CHAPTER 18

THE JET'S HOT BREATH

As MIKE flew south from Dayton in the roaring T-Bird his eyes scanned the countryside below for evidence of the blue Cessna. It was not always easy to see below, for the cockpit of the fighting jet did not allow a view of what was below, and Mike swung the ship from side to side so as not to miss any part of the ground he was passing over.

The jet was fast, too fast, Mike knew, for the job it was called upon to do. A survey of the ground to check each habitation and farm for the telltale spot of blue that would indicate the killer's plane needed a slower flying craft. A helicopter would have been ideal, but then it would have taken too long and it would not have been a match for the Cessna, should the latter take to the air.

He was in touch with the base every now and then and, as he swung around the area under suspicion, he had brief reports from the colonel. Johnny had come to and was recovering rapidly. The coffee had indeed been drugged—they had found the empty cup shoved out of sight in a corner of the locker room and a quick analysis had shown that some sort of sleeping pill had been dissolved in it.

Mike realized as he heard the report that he had clearly been included in the murder plot, for if he had also drunk the coffee, nothing would have saved the two Project Quicksilver candidates from a fiery and sudden death.

He gritted his teeth and renewed his careful probing of the ground below. He did not want to fly too low, for the noise of a fighting jet was often resented by the farmers. Nor could he fly very slowly without jeopardizing his stability. For a time he began to wonder if he was too late, or if the Cessna had been hidden too well.

It wouldn't do the killer any good if he just returned to his farm hideout and remained there. A convoy of armed Air Force Police was on its way by car to the place indicated. He'd be picked up for certain.

And then, swinging further south toward the Kentucky border, he saw a tiny moving spot low in the air—something flying south. Swiftly he banked the roaring T-Bird and shot down to investigate.

As he drew closer, he saw the spot grow into the shape of an airplane, a private, light-passenger airplane of the Cessna type. And it was blue!

He saw the blue Cessna!

Mike's T-Bird roared over the little plane and, as he banked for a turn around, Mike got a closer view. It was the Cessna, all right, and surely the same one that had crossed the camp at Mount Evans, the same that had been seen around Wright Field.

As the thundering jet-fighter roared overhead, the pilot of

the Cessna showed signs of concern. The little plane increased its speed, which at tops would not be much more than one hundred miles an hour, less than one sixth of the Air Force fighter's capacity. It drew closer to the ground surface as if daring the fast jet to come too close.

But Mike knew his T-Bird flying and he was an eagle seeking its prey. Again he bore down on the Cessna, flashed past this time only a few yards over it, swung around with a deafening roar that made the light little craft toss and shiver in the disturbed air currents.

Mike saw its pilot, and in a flash he recognized the thin gaunt features of the man who had impersonated a lieutenant. He even spotted the hooked scar across the man's cheek. The man must have suspected who was his tormentor in the jet, for he waved a fist at the T-33 as it went by, waved again to tell it to stay away.

Mike shook his head grimly. "You're going to come down, fellow, right down on the ground so the cops can get you," he whispered aloud.

Again he brought the thundering jet around behind the Cessna, flashed past him, this time so close that if the pilot had stood up in his seat he might have touched the racing silver bottom of Mike's fuselage. As Mike passed him, he swiftly pulled up, executed a near and steep climb so that the roaring hot exhaust of his raging jet stream would bathe the Cessna in its hot gases.

The killer knew what Mike was up to, but he was helpless to avoid it. All he could do was attempt to duck under the exhaust, to drive his light plane even closer to the ground.

Once again Mike roared around behind him, came up to repeat the maneuver, and again the now desperate killer-pilot found himself being forced closer and closer to the ground below.

A third time around, and Mike was grinning fiercely beneath the covering oxygen mask. "Down you go, down among the snakes where you belong!"

Already the trees and rocks of the Kentucky hillsides were very close, a hundred feet below. The blue plane tried to duck again, but the margin was now too close. As Mike once more roared overhead, once more threatened the Cessna with the T-Bird's jet stream, the blue plane was forced lower, and then ... a hillside rising above the trees ...

There was a crash. The blue plane struck the rising slope of the hill, performed a double somersault, its wings and tail

"You're going to come down, fellow," Mike said.

breaking apart. And then—when next Mike swung around and
rolled to see—there was a pile of wreckage bursting into flame,
a tearing scar in the grassy side, and the beginning of a surge
of smoke.

Of the pilot, Mike saw nothing. He swung away, called into
the base and reported the incident, giving the location of the
wreck as near as he could make out.

He roared back to Wright Field, and, as he went, he felt a curious reaction. He slumped down in his seat and let himself be overcome by a strange exhaustion. The heat of peril, the heat of anger, both of which had consumed him during the past hours, had worn themselves out. Now he felt sobered and silenced. Possibly he had taken a life, though it was not yet certain. If so, it was the life of one who had attempted to take his, not once but twice, and who had attempted to take the lives of others. The road to the stars may take some strange

123

turns, Mike thought, as he prepared for a landing at the base, and nothing should ever surprise me.

He realized that nobody yet knew this strange killer-pilot's motive, nor why he had staged the attacks he had. Until that motive was found, there would always be the need to watch out for new dangers.

Activities for Mike and Johnny were suspended for the rest of that day. But they took their weightlessness tests the next morning, for Johnny had made a complete and safe recovery. This time they went through the outlined maneuvers without a hitch.

Both young fliers reported the same sort of reactions that Mike had experienced the day before—a sense of well-being, a little tingling internally, and no aftereffects. Checking around among the other fellows afterward, Mike found that most of them had taken to the loss of gravity the same way. But there were others, some fellows who had complained of a sensation of falling or of feeling that they were standing on their heads during the period of weightlessness. These fellows had become a little dizzy during the time, had lost their appetites afterward, and had felt mildly airsick.

There were two among the candidates who became quite ill, had the symptoms of acute motion-sickness, had even been unable to hold down their meals, and had been sick for hours afterward.

It was unpleasantly obvious to Mike and his friends that these unfortunate candidates could never become space fliers, even though they might have qualified well on every other score. Just as there are people who cannot travel at sea, so apparently there are people who will never be able to stand space flight.

After Mike and Johnny had reported on their own sensations, they found that the tests were complete. Now they were on their own. They were told to hang around the base, but were given nothing more to do, while the Space Task Group studied their records and determined the results.

Of the pilot of the blue Cessna, nothing was found. The Air Police and the Kentucky troopers had searched the wreckage and the neighborhood, but no body was found. The man, certainly injured, had made good an escape. Still, Mike and the boys agreed that it was unlikely they'd see more of him for a long time.

CHAPTER 19

LADDER TO THE STARS

LATE one afternoon, a couple of days later, a messenger came to Mike as he was sitting and reading in the lounge of the Officers' Club. "Report to Colonel Drummond's office immediately, sir," the messenger said.

Mike got up, put away his book, and went with the messenger to the office the colonel had taken over in the Aeromedical Laboratories building. As he entered the room and came to attention snapping the colonel a smart salute, he saw that there were two other men sitting by the side of the colonel's desk. They were both men of the colonel's age, both in civilian clothes, and he had never seen them before. Nevertheless, there was something about them that suggested authority. They were surely men of ability and learning, and he knew instinctively that he was facing a dramatic moment in his young life.

"Sit down," the colonel said in a friendly tone. When Mike had complied he went on, "These gentlemen are with the National Aeronautics and Space Administration, even as I am, and we have been going over your tests. There's one thing we want to know, Mike, that isn't stated there."

He paused. In the back of his mind, Mike noted how the colonel had used his first name, informally. He leaned forward. "What is that, sir?" he asked.

One of the strangers leaned forward, looking hard into Mike's youthful features. "Tell us, just why do you want to be a space flier? After all, you must surely be aware that this work will be extremely dangerous. Do you realize that your chances of losing your life are very high? That many fine young men will be sacrificed, sometimes painfully, during the rocket experiments to come? There may be nothing in this for you but agony and sudden death. There won't be fame—not for those who must lose their lives during the next few years. Don't you want to live?"

Mike sat back in his seat and felt a sudden flush of blood rush to his face. He looked at the questioner and at the two others.

"Sirs, space flight means more to me than just a chance at fame. I know it's dangerous; I've thought about that since I was just a kid. I've wanted to cross space since I was old enough to recognize Mars and Venus and the constellations. I've never wanted anything else, and I know—I've studied and thought—about all the risks and dangers, and I still want to go.

"To me, sirs," he found himself leaning forward now, intense, anxious to convey to them the moving urge that overflowed his spirit, "the whole future of mankind is in the stars. We've explored the whole Earth; we can't go any further here and we've got to, you see, we've just got to. The stars, the other planets, are waiting for us and we've always wanted to go—the desire has never left us since the dawn of time. You can go back as far as you can in history, and men have always dreamed of conquering the stars.

"And now, sirs, right now, here in this very year, for the first time we can do it! We can go to the moon, we can reach the planets, here and now, just as surely as I'm sitting here. It's going to be done—and I want to be among those who do it. This means more to me than anything I can think of, sirs, believe me. I don't care if I die in the attempt—it would be an honor, and I won't be afraid of it—because this is the final triumph of human civilization, and it's greater than any one of us.

"I'm not asking for myself; I don't care if nobody ever hears of me, because I've never thought of it that way. But it's got to be done, and I happen to be here ready and willing to let you use me in whatever way I can to do it." He stopped, caught his breath.

"And then, again, sirs, you must know that our country's future depends on it. We've got to do it, for America's sake, and thereby for the whole world's sake, too. I joined the Air Force to serve my country to the best of my ability—and I think that, for me, space flying is truly the best for my ability."

He sat back, flushed a little, for the subject was one which had always deeply moved him. The three men who had been listening to him leaned back in their own chairs, stirred a little, exchanged looks.

Finally one took a sheet of paper from the desk, picked up a pen, and made a mark on the paper. He passed the paper to the other stranger and the action was repeated. The colonel took the document, looked at it, then added his own name. He looked at Mike and stood up.

Mike stood up, too. The colonel reached out a hand and

grasped Mike's hand. "Michael Alfred Robert Samson," he said, "I'm pleased to inform you that you have been chosen to be one of the seven United States astronauts of Project Quicksilver. You have my congratulations. The course you've picked out is going to be a hard one, but I think we can count on you."

Mike gulped, suddenly feeling weak in the knees. He accepted the colonel's handshake and those of the two other N.A.S.A. executives, thanked them in what he hoped was not a strained voice, and made his exit from the room.

As he closed the door behind him, he felt himself grabbed by both arms and lifted high. Cheers ripped through the anteroom. He felt himself being pounded and swung about by the strong arms of Johnny Bluehawk and Jack Lannigan. "You, too?" he asked, and they nodded exultantly.

Mike looked around at the rest of the fellows gathered there. There were four more, and that meant that all the astronauts were present. He knew them all, though not all had been in his particular testing squad.

There was Joseph Stacey of the Navy, and Orin McMahan, a Marine pilot. There was another Air Force man, Hart Williams, and there was one more—Rodney S. Harger, Jr., now smiling and nodding and appraising the others out of his pale, cold blue eyes.

As the seven went out together to have themselves a little celebration on the town before they settled down to the many months of hard, dangerous work to come, Mike's mind told him over and over again:

"I've made the first step up the ladder to the stars. Now— show me that second step."

At that moment, for Mike Mars, the second step was lying quietly in the darkness of a hangar beneath the hot sky of the most ominous desert in America. It was a strange, slender construction—a ship like no other anywhere in the world—a ship laden with peril, wild, untamed, still awaiting the hand of the man who could dare to call himself its master.

The story of that second step to the stars, of the task that awaited Mike Mars in the barren and inhospitable reaches of the Mojave Desert, will be found in the next book in this series of the conquest of space, *Mike Mars Flies the X-15*. Look for it.

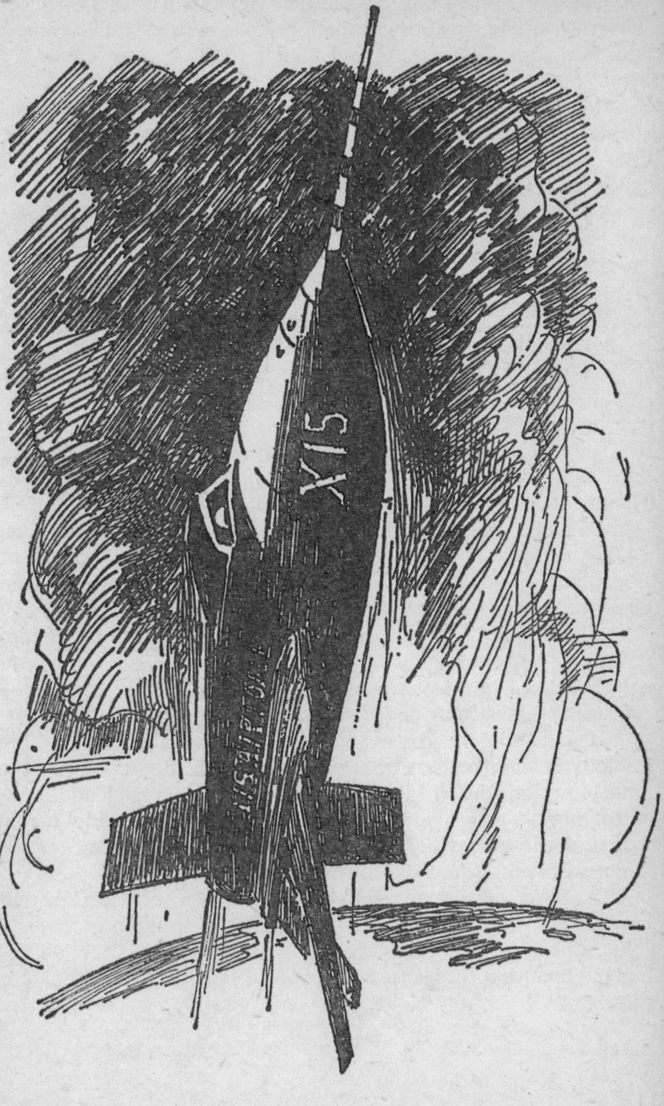
X15